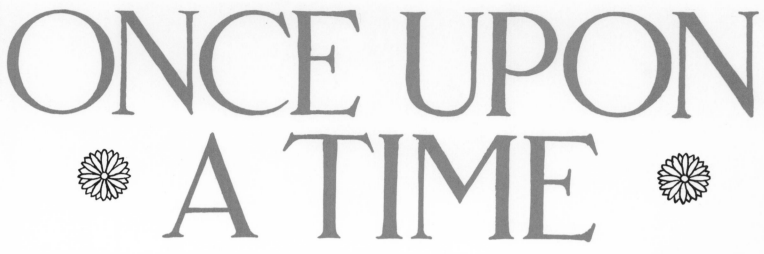

ONCE UPON A TIME

A BOOK OF OLD-TIME FAIRY TALES

Edited, with Introduction, by
KATHARINE LEE BATES
Professor of English Literature, Wellesley College

With Pictures by
MARGARET EVANS PRICE

CHECKERBOARD PRESS
NEW YORK

A LIST OF THE STORIES

1993 Edition
Illustrations copyright © 1921 Checkerboard Press, Inc.
Renewal copyright © 1949 Checkerboard Press, Inc. All rights reserved.
No part of this book may be reproduced or transmitted in any form or by any means,
electronic or mechanical, including photocopying, recording, or by any information
retrieval system without permission in writing from the publisher, Checkerboard Press, Inc.,
30 Vesey Street, New York, NY 10007. Printed in U.S.A. ISBN: 1-56288-256-2 X(1/20)
Library of Congress Catalog Card Number: 86-60224

 Printed on recycled paper.

THE TRUTH OF FAIRY TALES

IT is a pity, but there are people who say fairy tales are not true. These are people, if you take notice, who were children so long ago that they have forgotten how honest the looks of daisies are when, sitting on the ground, one's face is no higher than theirs, and how sweet is the chime of Canterbury bells when the little ringer stands below. It is a long, long time since they have talked with a Frog Prince on the edge of a well or danced their satin shoes into shreds for pure gladness of heart. There is a truth for childhood as well as a truth for tall, troubled daddies who have their own funny way of thinking pages of figures important. To the children these pages are foolish, scribbled over only by crooked little shapes marked in ink or pencil, pictures not nearly so amusing as the houses and boats and motor cars they scrawl with colored chalks on their own playroom blackboards. To the fathers, of course, the figures are not figures at all, but houses and boats and motor cars, bonds and bills, stocks and dividends. If fathers remembered the language of Fairyland, they could read to the children from those dismal account books of theirs the same old wonder stories all written carefully out in those crooked little shapes,—how, for instance, brave Jack Business had gone out to slay Giant Debt, Giant Mortgage, Giant Income Tax, and even that monstrous, many-headed ogre, Giant High Cost of Living.

If mere figures look like this to middle age, why may not childhood's brighter eyes see pink-skirted fairies dancing in the rosebushes, roguish elves plotting mischief under the brims of their straw-colored, sky-colored hats in the pansy bed, Rumpel-stilt-skin capering for joy of his secret, and dusty Hop-o'-My-Thumbs, that the gardeners call toads, hurrying by paths of their own back to their homes in the shade of lilac and laurel? And once outside the garden, how hill and fields and wood abound with

"Wee folk, good folk
Trooping all together,
Green jacket, red cap,
And white owl's feather!"

In Ireland even the grown-ups are friends with the fairies. "There is no man mowing the meadow but what sees the little people at one time or another."

Not true? Bless your heart! These tales have been true since the beginning of the world. The first duck that ever quacked was a Drakestail out for adventures. The first pumpkin that ever grew was a golden coach, waiting for Cinderella. And if, as all good gossips believe, telling a thing over and over makes it so, who can question the romance of the Little Ash Maiden, when no fewer than three hundred and forty-five different tellings of the story may be found written down in books to-day? These are tales of many nations, told in many languages, but they all agree about Cinderella and her lost slipper, though some say the slipper was glass and some say silver and some say fur and some say gold. They differ about Cinderella's helper, too. Sometimes it is a fairy godmother that comes stepping through the evening shadows, a tiny lady leaning on an ivory staff white as a wand of moonlight, but sometimes it is a kindly dove, or a strange green bird with a rare taste in toilets. Little girls over in Italy are told at bedtime, while the black lashes droop lower and lower over big black eyes, how the friendly green bird dressed Cinderella for her first ball in leaf-green with diamonds bright as dew, and for her second ball in sea-green with jewels as many-tinted as the foam, but for her third ball "in all the colors of the heavens; all the comets, the stars and moon on her dress, and the sun on her brow." No wonder the eyes of the young prince were dazzled!

And if the little Italian girls fall asleep dreaming of princely lovers, why not! Dreams are true, too, in their own beautiful way. What real boy, absorbed though he seems in fishing and baseball, does not sometimes, off on the hills with his dog, blush through the tan and freckles at his own dream, that dream he would not hint even to his mother for all of Captain Kidd's buried treasure, that dream of some day making gallant way through thorn and forest and finding the sleeping princess, Briar Rose, waiting for him in her enchanted garden?

Fairy tales not true! We live in their very midst. Never did hens lay such golden eggs as now. What seven-leagued boots can overtake the speed of the messages that are flashed about the globe? The blue air is crossed by flying chariots more marvelous than any the magician of Giant Galligantus could make. Many a princess in disguise, like Little Furball, and the queen of King Hawksbeak, and the Goose Girl, is doing her daily drudgery with a brave face. Still Rapunzel sings in her ivory tower. And Beauty still transforms the Beast into a Fairy Prince.

A fairy story is, after all, only a wonder story; and so all this wonderful world of ours is a gay-pictured fairy book. Our fathers and mothers of a thousand and two thousand and three thousand years ago knew this better than we do and stayed children all their lives, watching the glad ways of the wildwood. How often that runaway little lad, Will Shakespeare, spied on the dainty court manners of rich-mantled Moth and gold-helmed Mustardseed, of Pease-blossom —

> "Whose woven wings the summer dyes
> Of many colors,"

and of Cobweb, dressed very much like Tom Thumb,

> "His hat made of an oaken leaf,
> His shirt a spider's web!"

These child-hearted ancestors of ours, who dropped toads and diamonds from their lips just as we do, knew about witches and dragons, too, and were at home among the forest folk in fur and feathers. They delighted in the cleverness of Bre'r Rabbit and looked out for the tricks of Reynard the Fox. They were warned of the wickedness of the wolf by Little Red Riding Hood, for, with the cake and pat of butter fresh in her basket, she is still tripping all over Europe on her way to visit her Grandmother; and here in America the glint of her little hooded cloak, bright as a firefly, may be followed from the White Mountains to the Rockies, and from the Rockies to the Sierras and out beyond the Golden Gate, past the islands of the sea, back to the India where she began. Don't ever believe any one who tells you the wolf, however big his mouth, could truly eat up Red Riding Hood! Let no tender-hearted child grieve over her story, but be sure she found her way out of those grim jaws, Grandmother and butter and cake and all, and left the lying wolf to the stomach-ache he deserved. It is even rumored that the wolf was so ashamed of himself that he repented and turned into a collie, the most devoted of guardians for any Little Red Riding Hood who takes a lonely road.

It is clear that fairy tales are rich in the truth of imagination. They stand to a child's mind for that play which his elders call art. They are rich in sympathy, too, enlarging a child's circle of friends. Fairies are, as a rule, charming in their looks and manners, merry and sociable, eager to help people out of trouble. The bad fairy is only one whom some slight, like not being invited to the christening, has put out of temper. Even gnomes and goblins are full of fun, and the worst of ogres may have an amiable wife.

Fairy tales have moral and spiritual values. They quicken the budding spirit to beauty and joy, to the magic and mystery of earth; they condemn pride, envy, laziness, selfishness, cruelty; they honor pluck, patience, generosity, gentleness, mercy; they hold the divine faith that goodness cannot in the long run be overcome of evil. Children are quick to catch the noble strain even in the wildest of their fairy-tale heroes, whose exploits life will give them many a chance to emulate. That adventurous Jack the Giant-Killer did not kill all the giants. While Ogre Greed still gobbles his prey in his great guarded castle, there is fighting yet for every Jack Braveheart to do.

KATHARINE LEE BATES

I'LL GIVE YOU ALL THESE BEANS FOR YOUR COW

ONCE UPON A TIME

JACK AND THE BEANSTALK

Once upon a time there was a poor widow who had an only son, named Jack. He was good-natured and affectionate but lazy. As time went on, the widow grew poorer and poorer until she had nothing left but her cow. And all the time, it seemed, Jack grew lazier and lazier.

One day Jack's mother said to him: "Tomorrow you must take the cow to market. The more money you get for her the better for us, for we have nothing left to live on."

Next morning Jack got up earlier than usual, hung a horn around his neck, and started out with the cow. He was very happy at having such an important errand. On the way to market he met a queer little old man.

"Good-morning, my lad," said the queer little old man. "Where may you be going with that fine cow?"

"To market," replied Jack.

"And what may you be going to market for?" asked the queer little old man.

"To sell the cow," said Jack.

"As if you had wit enough to sell cows!" chuckled the queer little old man. "A lout of a lad that doesn't even know how many beans make five!"

"Two in each hand and one in your mouth," answered Jack, with a quickness that would have made his mother proud of him.

"Oho!" laughed the queer little old man. "Oho! Since you know beans, suppose you look at these," and he held out his hand, filled with sunrise-colored, sunset-colored, rainbow-colored beans. "I'll give you all these for your cow."

"That would be a good bargain," thought Jack; so he traded the cow for the beans, and hurried home to his mother. He could hardly wait to turn his pocket inside out and show her the treasure he had brought.

"Look," he said gleefully, as he poured the beans into her lap, "I got all these pretty beans for the cow."

"You stupid boy," cried his mother angrily. "Now we shall have to starve." And she flung the beans out of the open window.

There was no supper for Jack that night, and the next morning he woke early, feeling very hungry. But why was his room so dark? And what was that shadow across his window? Jack jumped out of bed and went to the window to find out. It seemed as if a tall tree grew where no tree had been before.

Jack ran into the garden and found that it was not a tree but a beanstalk! And such a beanstalk! It had sprung up during the night from the beans his mother had thrown out of the window, and had grown so quickly its top was out of sight.

Jack began to climb, and he climbed and he climbed and he climbed. All the time he grew hungrier and hungrier and hungrier. It was almost noon when he reached the top of the beanstalk and stepped off into the sky where all the grass is blue. There was not a person or a house or a tree in sight. Jack walked on and on and on until he met a beautiful woman with a face like a star. She was dressed in shining clothes, and she carried a wand on the top of which was a little gold peacock.

"Good-morning, Jack," was her greeting.

"How in the world does she know my name?" thought Jack to himself, but he only said, taking off his cap: "Good-morning, my lady."

Now the lady was a fairy and she knew what Jack was thinking, and answered him without his having to ask any questions.

"I know who you are," she said, "and where you come from, and how you got here. And I will tell you where you are and what you are to do."

Then she told Jack he was in a country that belonged to a wicked Giant. This Giant had killed Jack's father and stolen all his gold and precious things. Jack had been only a baby at that time and could not remember, and his mother had been too sad even to talk to him about it. But that was why she was poor.

"If you and your mother are ever to be happy again," said the fairy, "you must punish that Giant. It will not be an easy thing to do, but you will succeed if you are brave."

The fairy whispered in Jack's ear for a minute, telling him what to do. Then she left him and Jack walked on and on and on.

Toward evening he came to the door of a castle. He blew his horn, and a woman as broad as she was tall, opened the door. "I am very tired and hungry," said Jack politely. "Can you give me supper and a night's lodging?"

"You little know, my poor lad, what you ask," sighed the square woman. "My husband is a giant, and eats people. He would be sure to find you and eat you for his supper. No, no, it would never do!" And she shut the door.

But Jack was too tired to go another step, so he blew his horn again, and when the Giant's wife came to the door he begged her to let him in. The Giant's wife began to cry, but at last she led Jack softly into the castle. She took him past dungeons where men and women were waiting to be killed. Then they came to the kitchen, and soon Jack was enjoying a good meal and quite forgetting to be afraid. But before he had finished there came a thump, thump, thump of heavy feet, and in less than no time

the Giant's wife had popped Jack into the great oven to hide.

The Giant walked in sniffing the air. "I smell boy," he thundered.

"You are dreaming," laughed his wife, "but there is something better than dreams in this dish." So the Giant stopped sniffing and sat down to supper.

"Through a hole in the oven Jack peeped out and watched the giant eat. And how he did gobble! It seemed to Jack that no one, not even a giant, could possibly eat so much. When all the dishes were empty, the Giant bade his wife: "Bring me my hen."

She brought a much-ruffled hen and put it on the table.

"Lay," shouted the Giant, and the hen laid a golden egg.

"Another," roared the Giant, and the hen, though she had not done cackling over the first, laid another golden egg.

Again and again the Giant shouted his orders in a voice of thunder, and again and again the hen obeyed, till there were twelve golden eggs on the table. Then the Giant went to sleep, and snored so loud that the house shook.

When the biggest snore of all had shaken Jack out of the oven, he seized the hen and ran off as fast as he could. On and on and on he ran, until he reached the top of the beanstalk. He climbed quickly down, and carried the wonderful

hen, still cackling, to his mother. Day after day the hen laid its golden eggs, and by selling them Jack and his mother might have lived in luxury all their lives.

But Jack kept thinking about that wicked giant who had killed his father, and of the fairy's command. So one day he climbed the beanstalk again. When he reached the top he stepped off, followed the same path as before, and arrived at the Giant's castle. This time he had dressed himself to look like a very different person, as he did not want the Giant's wife to know him. And sure enough, when the square woman came to the door she did not recognize the lad she had hidden in the oven.

"Please," said Jack, "can you give me food and a place to rest? I am hungry and tired."

"You can't get in here," answered the Giant's wife. "Once before I took in a tired and hungry young runaway, and he stole my husband's precious hen that lays golden eggs."

But Jack talked to the Giant's wife so pleasantly that she thought it would be unkind to grudge him a meal. So she let him come in. After Jack had had a good supper the Giant's wife hid him in a big cupboard. And it was none too soon, either, for in stalked the Giant, thump, thump, thump, sniffing the air. "I smell boy," he bellowed.

"Stuff and nonsense," said his wife, as she placed his supper on the table.

After supper the Giant roared "Fetch me my money-bags."

His wife brought two heavy bags, one full of silver and one full of gold; and Jack, peeping out of the cupboard, said to himself: "Those were my father's money-bags." The Giant emptied the money out of the bags, counted it over and over again, and then put it back. Very soon he was fast asleep.

As soon as Jack heard the Giant's loud snores he stole out of the cupboard, snatched up the bags, and ran off as fast as he could. On and on he ran until he reached the top of the beanstalk. Then he dropped the money-bags into his mother's garden and climbed quickly down the beanstalk after them.

Jack and his mother were now as rich as the King and Queen, yet Jack felt that the Giant had not been punished enough yet. But it was some time before he dared climb again to the land at the top of the beanstalk.

At last, however, Jack made up his mind to disguise himself like a chimney sweep and see if he could persuade the Giant's wife to let him in

11

"Play!" commanded the Giant, and the harp began to play all by itself. Such lovely tunes Jack had never heard. It played and played until it played the Giant to sleep, and his snores drowned the sweet music. Then Jack jumped out from under the kettle, no blacker than he was himself, and seized the harp. But no sooner had he slung it up over his shoulder than it cried out: "Master, Master!" For it was a fairy harp.

Jack was frightened and ran for his life toward the top of the bean-stalk. He could hear the Giant running behind him, thump, thump, thump, but the Giant was so heavy he could not run very fast. Jack reached the top of the beanstalk and slid down it as quick as lightning, calling out as he went: "Mother, Mother! The axe, the axe!"

Jack's mother, holding out the axe, met him as he touched the ground. There was no time to lose, for the Giant was already half way down the beanstalk. It swayed and bowed under his weight. With one slashing blow Jack cut the beanstalk in two. There was a crash, and the Giant lay dead in the garden. Then Jack told his mother all the story, while the harp played a dirge for its old master. As for the wonderful beanstalk, it never grew again.

once more. He climbed the bean-stalk, followed the same path, and came to the castle door. The square woman did not know him, and he begged her for a night's lodging.

"No, no, no," she said, "you can't come in here. The last little beg-gars I took in were thieves. One stole the hen that laid the golden eggs, and the other stole the money-bags. No, no, you can't come in."

But Jack begged and begged, and at last the Giant's wife took pity on him, gave him his supper, and then turned over an empty kettle and hid him under it. Soon the Giant thumped in, sniffing the air, and roared out: "I smell boy."

"Boy?" laughed his wife. "You are always smelling boy." And she placed his supper on the table.

After supper the Giant shouted: "Fetch me my harp." And his wife brought in a beautiful harp with strings of pure gold.

THE FROG PRINCE

One evening a beautiful young princess went into a wood near her father's palace and sat down under an oak tree beside a spring of cool, clear water. She brought with her a golden ball, which was her favorite plaything, and she amused herself by tossing it up and catching it again as it fell. But one time she threw it so high that when the ball came down she could not catch it. It fell on a slope and rolled along until at last it slipped into the spring. The Princess jumped up and looked into the spring for the ball, but the water was very deep — so deep and dark she could not see the bottom. Then she began to weep and sobbed,

"Oh! Oh! if I could only get my gold ball again, I would give all my fine clothes and my pearls and diamonds — everything I have in the world!"

Just as she said this, a big green frog stuck its head out of the spring and asked: "Beautiful Princess, why do you weep?"

"Alas!" said the Princess, "what good can it do to tell you, you old waddler? You cannot help me. My golden ball has fallen into the spring."

"I do not want your pearls and diamonds and fine clothes," croaked the frog, "but if you will love me and let me live with you in the palace and eat from your little gold plate and sleep on your little white pillow, I will bring you your ball again."

"What a silly frog!" thought the Princess. "He is as foolish as he is ugly. He can never climb out of the spring and up the steps of the palace. But perhaps he can get my ball again, so I had better promise him whatever he wants." Then she said to the frog: "If you will bring me my ball from the spring, I promise to do everything you ask."

Without a splash the frog dived deep into the spring. The Princess was still staring at the place where he sank, when he popped his green head out of the water and, sure enough, the ball was in his mouth. He tossed it out on the ground and the young Princess ran to pick it up. She was so happy to have it in her hand again that she never gave one thought to the frog, but ran home as fast as she could. The frog called after her in his hoarse voice: "Wait, wait, Princess. Take me with you, do!" But the Princess did not stop to say a word—not even "thank you."

Next day, just as the Princess sat down to dinner, she heard a strange noise, flop, flop, flop, slowly coming up the marble staircase. Soon after there came a thump low down at the door, and a hoarse voice said:

"Beautiful Princess, open your door,
That I may come in and go out no more.
Have you forgotten the vows you made
By the woodland spring, in the oak tree's shade?"

The Princess jumped down from her chair and ran and opened the door, and there at her feet sat the frog! She had forgotten all about him and was dreadfully frightened when she saw his fat green body and his wide mouth that was trying to smile. Shutting the door in his face, she came back to her seat.

"Who was it, daughter?" asked the King. "What has frightened you?"

"There is an ugly frog at the door," said she, "and he wants to come in. Last night I dropped my golden ball in the spring, and he dived down and brought it out for me. I promised him that he might live with me here and be my playmate, but I felt sure that he could never, never get out of the spring. And now he is at the door and I am afraid!"

Just then there came another thump, and the frog croaked:

"Beautiful Princess, open your door,
   That I may come in and go out no
      more.
   Have you forgotten the vows you
      made
   By the woodland spring, in the oak
      tree's shade?"

The King said kindly but very firmly to his daughter: "Princesses never break their word. You have made a promise and now you must keep it. Run and let him in."

So the Princess opened the door, and the frog came hop, hop, hopping into the room and up to her chair.

"Pick me up and put me on the table at your side," said he to the Princess, and the Princess dared not refuse. When he had settled himself on the table, the frog said: "Push your gold plate closer to me, that I too may eat out of it." The Princess shuddered but she pushed her plate closer, refusing to eat any more from it herself. When the frog had finished dinner, he said: "I am tired and sleepy; it is far from the well to the palace and the steps are steep. Carry me upstairs and put me on your little white pillow."

And the Princess, hating to touch the clammy creature, took him up between her thumb and finger and carried him upstairs. There she laid him on the pillow of her little bed, but when she laid her own head on the pillow, and the cold frog tumbled against her cheek, her patience left her and she flung him with all her might against the wall.

When he fell down, there was no frog at all, but a handsome young when they looked out into the moonlight there was a crystal carriage drawn by eight white horses decked with plumes of snowy feathers and with silver harness. And on the carriage was the Prince's coachman, who had bewailed the loss of his master so long and so bitterly that his heart had well-nigh burst. He had had to put three strong iron bands about it, lest it should break from grief and pain, but as they all set out merrily for the Prince's kingdom, crack, crack, crack went the iron bands, for the heart of the coachman, swelling with joy, had snapped them one after another.

prince stood beside her bed, looking at her with the most grateful eyes that ever were seen.

"Who are you? And where is the frog?" cried the Princess.

"An angry witch changed me to a frog," said the Prince, "and doomed me to remain a frog until some princess should let me eat from her plate and rest on her pillow. This wicked spell," he went on, "you have broken. And now will you marry me and go with me to my father's kingdom? I will love you and be good to you as long as I live."

The Princess, you may be sure, said yes without stopping long to think it over. Just then they heard a prancing in the courtyard, and

KING HAWKSBEAK

Once upon a time there was an old King who had only one daughter. He was very anxious that his daughter should marry, but while she was more beautiful than words can tell, she was so proud and rude that no man who came to woo her was good enough for her. She sent away one after another and even made fun of them to their faces.

One day her father gave a great feast and invited to it all the young bachelors of royal or noble blood from far and near. After the feast they were all lined up in a row according to their rank—first kings, then princes, then dukes, earls, and barons. The Princess was led down the line and told to choose a husband, but she carried her head high and found something wrong with every one.

The first was too fat. "You're too chubby, too round and tubby," she sneered. The next was too tall. "Long and lean, close and mean!" The third was too short. "Stout and short, not my sort!" The fourth was too pale. "What a gawk! White as chalk!" The fifth, who kissed the hem of her dress, was too red. "Don't peck my frock, you turkey-cock!" The sixth was not straight enough to suit her. "Why should

THE PRINCESS AND THE RAGGED BALLAD-SINGER

I pick a crooked stick?" So she went down the line making her saucy rimes. But she saved her choicest mockery for one young king who was the wonder of the world for beauty and strength, but whose nose was the least bit hooked. He would have asked her to be his queen, but she brushed rudely by him with the rime:

"Why should I stay for the silly talk
Of one whose nose is the beak of a
hawk?"

After that he was always called King Hawksbeak.

When the old King saw that his daughter only made fun of all her fine suitors, he was very angry. "By my beard," he swore, "the first beggar who comes to the door shall be her husband!"

Only a few days later a strolling ballad-singer took his stand under one of the castle windows and sang his best in hope of alms. When the King heard him, he said: "Let the fellow come up here." So the beggar was brought in, ragged, stooping, with wild hair, and whiskers that almost hid his face. He sang to the King and the Princess all the ballads he knew and then held out his torn hat for coppers, or perhaps a bit of silver.

The King said: "Your song has pleased me so much that I will give

you instead of money this daughter of mine for your wife."

The Princess cried out in disgust and dismay. But the King said: "I have sworn by my beard that you, too proud for royal suitors, should marry the first beggar who came to the door. That oath cannot be broken."

This king could be very stern when he chose, and the tears of his daughter did not move him. The court chaplain was called in and the Princess and the beggar were married then and there.

And then, although his daughter clung to his knees, the King shook her off. "Now you are a beggar-woman, and beggar-women do not live in palaces. Go hence with your husband."

19

The ballad-singer took his bride by the hand and led her out of the castle; she who had never before set sandal to the ground had to go with him on foot.

They came to a beautiful, leafy wood, and the Princess asked:

"Who is the lord of this forest so
    fine?"
"It belongs to King Hawksbeak.
    It might have been thine."

"Oh, I was a proud and foolish
    young thing.
  I would I had wedded that glori-
    ous King."

Soon afterward they reached a wide meadow, and she asked again:

"Who is the lord of these meadows
    so wide?"
"They belong to King Hawksbeak,
    who sought you for bride."

"Oh, I was a proud and foolish
    young thing.
  I would I had wedded that glori-
    ous King."

Then they passed through a large town, and again she asked:

"Who owns this city so thronging
    with life?"
"It belongs to King Hawksbeak,
    who wished you for wife."

"Oh, I was a proud and foolish
    young thing.
  I would I had wedded that glori-
    ous King."

"Enough of this!" exclaimed the beggar. "Why should you be wanting another husband? Am I not good enough for you?"

But the poor Princess, who had been so sharp of tongue, said never a word. She did not speak again until they came to a miserable hovel, when she cried out:

"This wretched hut, this cabin, to
    be mine!
  He's better housed who feeds my
    father's swine!"

The begger answered: "This is my house and yours. Here we are to live together and I hope you'll be content."

The door was so low that she had to bend her haughty head to enter. All was dark and empty within.

"Where are the servants?" she asked.

"Servants, indeed!" laughed the beggar. "Do you forget whose wife you are? If you want anything done, do it yourself. Light the fire and put the kettle on to get my supper. I am hungry."

But the Princess knew nothing about lighting fires or even putting on the kettle, and so to have any supper the ballad-singer had to do the work with his own hands, that were not so very skillful about it, either.

It did not take long to eat the black bread and cabbage soup which was all they had for supper. The bed was of straw, with a log of wood for a pillow, but the Princess was so tired she slept soundly, and was by no means ready to waken when the beggar made her get up. All day long he kept her busy scrubbing the poor house.

They lived like this for a few days, until their bread and cabbages were all gone.

Then the beggar said: "Wife, this won't do any longer; we can't live here without working. You shall make baskets."

So he went out and cut some rushes, and dumped them down before her. The Princess began to weave them as best she could, but

the stiff rushes bruised her tender hands.

"You cannot weave," said the beggar in a tone of disgust. "You would much better spin; any woman can do that."

Then the poor Princess sat down at the broken old wheel and tried to spin, but the harsh yarn cut her delicate fingers and made them bleed.

"Now," said the beggar angrily, "you see what a good-for-nothing you are. I have made a bad bargain in you. But sitting in the market place will not be too difficult even for you. I will get some crockery and you shall offer it for sale."

"Alas! how can I do that?" thought the unhappy Princess. If those before whom I have held my head so high should come and see me sitting in the market place offering pots for sale, it would be their turn to scoff." But she dared not disobey her husband, for fear he would leave her to die of hunger.

Her first day in the market place was not so bad. The people willingly bought of her because she was so beautiful, and they paid what she asked for her wares—nay, some even gave her the money and left her the pots as well.

She and the ballad-singer, who did nothing but sit on the doorstep

in the sun, lived on the gains as long as they lasted, and then the beggar laid in a new stock of cups and plates and pots and jars. The Princess took her seat at the entrance of the market and began to cry her wares in a low voice. But before she had sold a thing, a soldier on horseback came galloping up and rode right over her crockery. Crash! Crash! Cups and plates and pots and jars were broken into a thousand bits.

The Princess began to cry, and was so dismayed that she stopped only to pick up the two unbroken pots. "What will my husband say to me?" she cried. Home she ran, and with tears and trembling she told her story.

"Stupid! Who would ever think of sitting at the entrance of the market with crockery?" he said. "Stop that crying. I see you are no manner of use for any decent kind of work. I have been to our King's palace and asked if they do not want a kitchen drudge, and they promised to try you. You will get scraps enough to feed us both, at any rate."

So the Princess became kitchen drudge in King Hawksbeak's palace, and she had to wait upon the cook and do all the dirty work. At her husband's bidding she hung from her waist, one at each side, their two unbroken pots, and in

them took home all the scraps and leavings. On these they lived, and many a crust and many a rind did the Princess gnaw which she would scarcely have thrown to a dog in the days of her pride.

One morning she heard that the sister of the young King was to be married that evening. The cook made her stay late to help, but at last gave her a few moments of freedom, and she dragged herself upstairs and stood behind a door to peep at all the splendor.

When the rooms were lighted with their thousands of candles, and she saw the guests streaming in, each one more beautiful than the last, she thought with heavy heart of her sad lot, but she blamed only herself for the pride and rudeness which had lost her such happiness and brought her to such trouble.

Now and then the upper servants, as they passed, threw her bits from the savory dishes they were carrying away from the feast, and these she put into her pots to take home.

All at once, just as the dancing began, a splendid lord came in. He was dressed in silk and velvet, and wore a gold chain about his neck. He spied the beautiful woman who was hiding behind the door, seized her by the hand and, though making a wry face at her shabby gown, asked her to dance with him.

The Princess shrank back and shook her head. Her first glance told her it was King Hawksbeak, who had been one of her suitors and whom she had driven away with scorn and insult. But kings are used to having their own way. He laughed and drew her out into the middle of the ballroom. The string by which the pots were suspended at her sides broke; down fell the pots, shattered to pieces, and the chicken bones and edges of pie crust were spilled all over the ballroom floor.

When the guests saw this they burst into shouts of mocking mirth. The Princess was so ashamed she would gladly have sunk into the earth. Through the door and down the stairs she dashed, but running feet came after her and a strong arm held her fast. When she looked at her captor, she saw it was King Hawksbeak.

He spoke to her tenderly and said: "Do not be afraid of me. My hair is cut and my whiskers are gone. I am King Hawksbeak. I was the beggar who married you. I was also the soldier who rode over your crockery. For love of you have I done these things that your beauty might be made perfect by sympathy and gentleness. Forgive me, my Queen, for all I have let you suffer."

She wept bitterly and said: "I was very wicked, and I am not worthy to be your wife."

But he answered: "Be happy! Those evil days are over,—all left behind us with our broken pots. Now we will celebrate our true wedding."

Then came the waiting-women, who clad her in bridal raiment, and her father with all his court rode through the palace gate and wished her joy on her marriage with King Hawksbeak. Her father never told her whether he knew who the ballad-singer was. Did he?

DRAKESTAIL

Drakestail was a tiny little fellow. That is why he was given his name of Drakestail. But he had brains enough to fill a big, big head, and he made his brains work for him so hard that before he was very old he had saved a hundred round silver dollars.

Now the King of the country never saved anything, but spent his own money and everybody else's that he could lay his hands on. He heard that Drakestail had money, and rode in his own chariot to borrow it. And you may be sure that Drakestail bragged more than once that he had lent money to the King.

But a year went by, and a year and a day, and the King had not paid back the money nor even a cent of interest; so Drakestail began to feel it was not a good investment. He was a brave little duck, as brave as he was clever, and he finally made up his mind to call on the King and ask for the return of his round silver dollars.

So one fine spring morning, in his best suit of glossy green feathers, Drakestail started for the King's castle, chanting in his flat voice, "Quack, quack, quack! when shall I get my money back?"

25

He had not gone far when he met Slyboots, the Fox, prowling about to see what he could find.

"Good morrow, Neighbor Drakestail," said the Fox. "And whither away so bright and gay?"

"I am going to the King to get my money back."

"And may I go with you to the King?"

"One can't have too many friends," said Drakestail to himself. To the Fox he said: "You may go, but four legs tire sooner than two legs. Make yourself quite small, slip down my throat and into my gizzard, and I will carry you."

"Clever Drakestail!" chuckled Slyboots, the Fox. And bag and baggage he popped into Drakestail's broad yellow bill and was gone like a letter into a post box.

Again Drakestail set off, fresh as a spring breeze, still chanting his funny song. "Quack, quack, quack! when shall I get my money back?"

He had not gone far when he met Lady Leaning Ladder with her feet on the ground and her head leaning against the wall.

"Good morrow, Duckie Drakestail," said Lady Leaning Ladder. "And whither bound, so plump and round?"

"I am going to the King to get my money back."

"And may I go with you to the King?"

"One really can't have too many friends," said Drakestail to himself. To Lady Leaning Ladder he said: "You may go, but wooden feet tire sooner than web feet. Make yourself quite small, slip down my throat and into my gizzard, and I will carry you."

"Wise Drakestail!" creaked Lady Leaning Ladder. And as nimble as though she had joints she was into his bill and down his throat to keep company with Friend Fox.

With a "Quack, quack, quack," Drakestail set off again, chanting more cheerily than ever. A little farther on he met his sweetheart,

Rippling River, wandering quietly along through shade and sunshine.

"Welcome, welcome!" murmered Rippling River.

"Will you play at waterfalling?
Will you paddle a leaf canoe?

Or is something calling, calling,
Calling down the road to you?"

"I am going to the King to get my money back."

"And may I go with you to the King?"

"One really can't have too many friends," said Drakestail to himself. To Rippling River he said: "You may go, but silver sandals tire sooner than these brave red shoes of mine. Slip down my throat and into my gizzard and I will carry you."

"Wonderful Drakestail!" crooned Rippling River. And with all her rushes and lilies she slipped glug, glug, glug, into the yellow bill and down the narrow way and took her place between Friend Fox and Lady Leaning Ladder.

"Quack! Quack!" Drakestail once more was on the road. Just around the turn he met Buzzy Wasp's-nest, drilling his wasps in squads and battalions.

"Greetings, Friend Drakestail!" said Buzzy Wasp's-nest. "Whither and why, so spruce and so spry?"

"I am going to the King to get my money back."

"And may I go with you to the King?"

"One can't have too many friends," said Drakestail to himself. To Buzzy Wasp's-nest he said: "You may, but gauze wings tire sooner than these firm legs of mine. Make yourself quite small, slip down my throat and into my gizzard, and I will carry you."

"Marvelous Drakestail!" hummed Buzzy Wasp's-nest.

And to the rear, marching, he led his rank and file to join the others. Quarters were a little crowded now, but they didn't mind squeezing.

And Drakestail set off again— "quack, quack, quack!"

And now here is the capital and here is Quality Street, and who is it waddling up the sidewalk, quacking all the way,—who but Drakestail? Hopping up the steps of the King's palace he goes, chanting: "Quack, quack, quack! when shall I get my money back?"

"Rap! Rap!" That is the brass knocker which Drakestail handles none too gently.

"Who is there?" That is the porter, his head thrust out of the little side gate he calls the wicket.

"'T is I, Drakestail. I must speak to the King."

"Speak to the King! Speak to the King! More easily said than done. The King is now dining off pease-pudding and plums, and will not be disturbed."

"Tell him that it is I, and I have come he well knows why."

Bang goes the wicket, and away goes the porter to speak to the King.

Now the King had just sat down to dinner with all his ministers, and the royal chamberlain was tying a napkin around the King's neck.

"Good!" said the King, when the porter told his story. "I know who it is. Let him come in, and turn him into the barnyard with the other fowl."

Down comes the porter and opens the gate.

"Have the grace to enter."

"Good!" says Drakestail to himself. "I shall now see how they eat pease-pudding at court."

"This way, this way," said the porter. "This is the way they go who wish to see the King. And here you are, sir!"

"But this—this is the poultry yard!" You may imagine that Drakestail was in a rage.

"They will, will they?" said he. "But I'll never stop here; the King shall see me, that he shall. Quack, quack, quack, when shall I get my money back?"

Now chickens like chickens, and turkeys like turkeys, and geese like geese, but Drakestail was not turkey nor chicken nor goose, and they began to make fun of his tiny body no bigger than a duck's tail.

"Who is this absurd little creature?" they asked. "And why is he not happy here in the royal poultry yard? Let's peck him to death."

And they rushed at him, cackling and gobbling and hissing in a truly awful fashion.

"Good-by, Drakestail!" said Drakestail to himself. But just then Friend Fox popped into his mind, and he cried:

"Slyboots, Slyboots, come out of
    my gizzard,
  Or Drakestail will die in this
    barnyard blizzard."

Then Slyboots, the Fox, sprang out, rushed at the astonished chickens, geese, and turkeys and sent them all scurrying under the royal barn. Not one remained in sight. And Drakestail, his worries over, began to chant at the top of his voice: "Quack, quack, quack! when shall I get my money back?"

When the King, who was still at table, heard this saucy song and when the poultry keeper told him how his chickens, geese, and turkeys had been driven under the barn, he turned red in the face with wrath.

"Throw this tail of a drake into the well, and make an end of him," he cried.

The servants rushed to carry out his command, as kings' servants always do. In the well Drakestail swam round and round and thought it over. He wasn't afraid of drowning, but he saw no way of getting out of such a deep hole. But wait! There was Lady Leaning Ladder.

"Ladder, Ladder, come out of
    my gizzard.
  Can a duck climb a slippery wall
    like a lizard?"

Leaning Ladder hastened out and placed her two arms on the edge of the well. Then Drakestail waddled up as best he could, and with a flurry of feathers landed in the yard, and began to chant louder than ever: "Quack, quack, quack! when shall I get my money back?"

When the King, who was still at table and laughing heartily at the joke he had played on Drakestail, heard him still singing about his money, he turned white in the face with rage.

"Heat a furnace," he cried, "and throw this tail of a drake into it. Is he a wizard that he plays such tricks?"

The furnace was soon red hot and the servants seized the duck to throw him into it. But this time Drakestail was not afraid. He counted on his sweetheart, Rippling River.

> "River, River, come out of my
>   gizzard.
>   With you to help me, I'll play
>   the wizard."

Rippling River came flowing forth, and sizz-z-z, fizz-z-z — the furnace fire

was out. Then she flooded the hall of the palace to the height of more than four feet.

And Drakestail, free from his worry, swam on her breast, chanting at the top of his voice: "Quack, quack, quack! when shall I get my money back?"

The King was still at table and thought himself well rid of Drakestail, but when he heard that song and knew that even a fiery furnace could not harm Drakestail, he sprang up from the table brandishing the carving knife.

"Bring him here and I'll cut his throat! Bring him here quick!" cried he.

And two footmen ran to fetch Drakestail.

"At last," said Drakestail proudly, as he hopped up the great stairs, "the King has decided to receive me."

But he almost died of fright when he waddled into the room and saw the King, purple with anger, standing with knife in hand. And all the ministers had their knives in their hands. "It is the end," thought Drakestail. Just then he remembered that he had one friend left, and he cried feebly:

> "Wasp's-nest, Wasp's-nest, come out of
>   my gizzard.
>   Come quick, before my throat is
>   scissored!"

And then! "B-z-z-z! B-z-z-z! At them, boys! At them!" Buzzy Wasp's-nest rushed out with all his wasps. The wasps buzzed about the heads of the King and his ministers, and stung them so fiercely that they were quite beside themselves. Not knowing where to hide, they jumped helter-skelter from the window and broke their necks on the courtyard pavement.

And there stood Drakestail, his four loyal friends about him, in the big dining hall!

And his song changed. "Quack, quack, quack!" he chanted. "Now I shall get my money back." He hunted and he hunted and he hunted in all the drawers and all the cupboards and all the closets, but not one cent could he find. His hundred round silver dollars had been spent—all spent.

As he waddled from room to room he came at last to the great hall where the throne stood. He was tired and hopped up on the throne to think. Meanwhile the people had found their King and his ministers quite, quite dead in the courtyard, and they came rushing into the palace to see what had happened. Through the palace they poured and at length they came to the throne-room. And there on the throne sat Drakestail! You may imagine that

he was surprised when he heard them shout:

"The King is dead, long live the King!
Heaven has sent us down this thing."

By the time the shouting had died away, Drakestail was over his surprise and bowed majestically to the people, just like a real king. There were some who grumbled that they did not want a Drakestail to rule over them, but those who knew Drakestail said he would make a far better king than the spendthrift who lay dead below. So they took the crown off the fallen King's head and set it on Drakestail's head, and it fitted him like wax.

And so Drakestail became king.

The crowning over, he said, "Let's go to supper, Rippling River, Lady Leaning Ladder, Buzzy Wasp's-nest, Friend Fox, and all. I'm so hungry!"

THE CROSS FAIRY'S GIFT TO THE PRINCESS

BRIAR ROSE OR THE SLEEPING BEAUTY

Once upon a time there lived a King and Queen who grieved because they had no child. Finally a daughter was born to them, and the King was so happy that he gave a great christening feast. As godmothers for his little daughter he asked all the fairies but one in the kingdom. Seven he asked, but the bad-tempered fairy he left out. He hoped that each, after the fairy custom, would give the Princess a gift.

From the christening the company returned to the palace, where a splendid feast had been prepared. Before each fairy was placed a crinkled emerald plate, like a clover leaf, set with diamonds like dewdrops. Just as they were taking their places at the table, in came the cross fairy who had not been invited. She rode into the hall on a snap-dragon, for the slight had made her crosser than ever. The King had a plate of pure pearl like a lily petal set before her, but she angrily pushed it away and looked enviously at the emerald plates, which had been made to order for the seven fairies. The cross fairy thought her-self ill-treated, and muttered threats under her breath. One of the wisest fairies, who was seated near her, heard these threats, and felt sure she meant to do some harm to the little Princess.

When the company rose from the table, this wise fairy hid behind the cradle, that she might speak last and perhaps undo some of the harm which she knew was brewing in the bad-tempered fairy's mind.

Now the fairies began to give their gifts to the Princess. The youngest gave her beauty; the next, wit; the third, grace; the fourth, virtue; the fifth, a lovely voice; the sixth, a smile to win all hearts.

Then it was the cross fairy's turn. With her ivory wand pointed like a spear at the royal baby, she cried out:

"The King's daughter in her rose-bud youth shall prick her hand with a spindle, and fall down dead!"

Everybody fell a-crying with fright at this terrible gift, and as for the poor Queen, she instantly fainted away. But just then the wise fairy popped up from behind the cradle and said: "Be comforted, O King! Revive, O Queen! My gift is still to with her maids. While the maids were enjoying a gossip with the gardeners, the Princess went roaming about the palace, exploring one room after another. At last she came to an old tower, and at the top of the tower she found a little room in which an old woman sat busily spinning. This old woman had never heard of the King's proclamation.

"Good day, granny!" said the Princess. "What are you doing?"

"I am spinning, my pretty lass," said the old woman, who did not recognize her.

"That is charming!" the Princess cried. "How do you do it? Let me see whether I can spin!"

She caught at the whirling spindle. But because she was too eager, or because a fairy's decree *must* be fulfilled, the spindle pricked her hand and she dropped to the floor in a faint.

The old woman, greatly alarmed, cried for help. People came running from all sides. The gardeners threw water in the face of the Princess. The maids loosened her clothes, and beat her hands, and bathed her temples, but nothing could rouse her.

Then the King and Queen, who had heard the alarm, came too. They knew at once the fairy's evil wish had been fulfilled. They had the Princess carried to a most beautiful

come. I cannot undo entirely what this unkind fairy has done. Your daughter will prick her hand with the spindle and fall to the floor, but instead of dying she will sink into a deep sleep which will last a hundred years. From that sleep, when her dream is over, a king's son shall waken her."

Yet the King hoped to save his dear child from the threatened evil; so he had his heralds proclaim that no one in all the country should spin, or even have a spindle in the house, on pain of death.

When the Princess was fifteen or sixteen years old, the King and Queen went one day to one of their country houses, leaving the Princess room, deep in the heart of the palace, and laid on a bed decked with rose and silver coverlets.

She might have been an angel as she lay there, for her deep sleep had not driven away her lovely color. Her cheeks and lips were as pink as briar roses, her forehead fair as a lily. Her eyes were closed but she breathed softly, and it was easy to see that happy dreams played beneath her eyelids. The King commanded that she be left to sleep in peace until the hour of her awakening had come.

Now the wise fairy whose quick wit had saved the life of the Princess, was thousands of miles away,

but she knew what had happened and came at once in her chariot of golden fire, drawn by eagles. She was afraid the Princess would be frightened and lonesome if she should awaken all alone in an empty, crumbling castle. So this is what she did.

She touched with her wand everything and everybody about the palace, except the King and Queen. She touched the governesses and the ladies in waiting, the gentlemen, the officers, the stewards, cooks, guards, and pages; she touched those weeping maids and shame-faced gardeners; she touched the horses in the stables, the great mastiff in the yard, and the Princess's tiny poodle which lay on the bed beside her. And as she touched them they all fell asleep, not to waken until their mistress should wake, so that they might all attend upon her. Even the fire slept, and the spit that stood before it full of half-roasted partridges and pheasants. It all took but a moment, for the fairies work quickly.

Then the King and Queen, having kissed their daughter, left the hushed palace. The King issued a new proclamation, forbidding anyone to approach its gates, but such laws were not needed, for in half an hour there had sprung up about the palace a hedge of thorny shrubs, and year by year these grew into trees so thick and high that neither beast nor man could force a way through.

The castle itself was hidden. Only the top of the tower could be seen from a distance.

On the very day that the hundred years ended, the son of the king then reigning was a-hunting, and spied the tower beyond the thorny wood. He asked what it was, and many strange stories were related, but finally an old peasant told him the true tale of the sleeping princess and of the king's son who was to waken her. The Prince felt very sure, from the way his heart began beating, that *he* was the king's son who was to have that wonderful adventure, and he set out at once for the wood. And when he reached it the great trees and the thorns opened of their own accord to let him pass, but closed behind him, so that even his companions could not pass through.

He came at last to the courtyard of the palace, over which hung an utter silence. Nothing living was to be seen but men and animals in profound slumber. The Prince crossed the court and mounted the stairs. In the guard room, fast asleep, the guards stood drawn up in line. Indeed, in every room that he entered he found men and women, some standing, some sitting, often with smiling lips but always with closed eyes.

On he went and on to the very heart of the palace, where, in a beautiful room of gold, he saw the loveliest sight in the world—a sleeping princess, a statue in rose and silver, so fair she seemed an angel. He fell on his knees beside her, and looked at her in awe.

Just at that moment the enchantment came to an end. The Princess opened her eyes and saw her dream before her. She smiled on the kneeling youth and said:

"Is it you, my Prince? I have waited long."

They talked for hours, and still had not said half that was in their hearts to say. Meanwhile, everything in the palace waked with the Princess, and everyone took up his task just where he had left it. At nightfall a lady in waiting courtesied to the Princess and announced that supper was served. And after supper the King's son led his bride, in her gorgeous robes of a hundred years ago, to the royal chapel, where they were married by the very priest who had married the father and mother of the Princess.

The next morning the bridegroom and bride left the palace and passed through the dark, gloomy wood into the bright sunshine of the world beyond. And when the Princess turned to look at the castle where she had slept so many years, behold, castle and wood had vanished, and they stood on an open plain.

So the Princess rode with her Prince to his father's court, and there they lived ever after a life as happy as her dream.

FURBALL MADE READY TO SLIP OUT INTO THE WORLD

FURBALL

Once upon a time there was a Princess whose hair was of pure gold. She was the most beautiful maiden on earth and as good as she was beautiful. But she was often sad because her mother had died. Her father, the King, promised her hand to an Ogre, who in return agreed to give the King fifty wagons of silver.

When the Princess heard of her father's bargain she was greatly alarmed, and begged him not to make her so unhappy. But nothing could change his mind. His daughter, however, had quick wits and she said to her father: "Before I marry I must have three bridal gifts—a dress as golden as the sun, another as silvery as the moon, and a third as glittering as the stars. I shall want, besides, a coat made of a thousand different kinds of fur. Every animal in the kingdom must give a part of his skin to make that coat."

"There!" she thought, "I have asked for things which he cannot get, and so he will have to give up his wicked plan."

But the King at once began to provide for the bridal gifts. The most skillful weavers in all the land were sent for and ordered to weave the three dresses, one to be as golden as the sun, another as silvery as the moon, and a third as glittering as the stars. Hunters were sent into the forest to kill wild animals and bring home their skins, of which the coat was to be made. At last, when they were all ready, the King laid them before his daughter and said: "To-morrow your marriage shall take place."

Then the poor Princess saw there was no hope of changing her father's heart, and that her only way of escape from the Ogre was to run away.

In the night, when all the castle was still, she rose from her bed. The sun, moon, and star dresses she folded into a packet so small that she could shut them up in a walnut shell. Then she put on the fur coat, stained her face and hands dark brown with walnut juice, and slipped out into the world.

After traveling all night, she came just at dawn to a large forest. She was very tired, so she crept into a hollow tree and went to sleep. The sun rose higher and higher but still she slept on, and did not awake until nearly noon.

Now on this very day the young King to whom the wood belonged was hunting in the forest. His hounds came to the tree where the Princess slept, and began to sniff about and run round and round the tree, barking eagerly. The King called to his hunters and said: "Look sharp, and see what sort of game hides in that hollow tree."

Two hunters ran to see. When they came back, they told the King that in the hollow tree there was the most wonderful creature ever seen. "It is sound asleep," they

said, "and its body is covered with a thousand different kinds of fur."

"Go and see," said the King, "whether you cannot capture it alive. Bind it on the wagon and bring it to the castle."

While the hunters were binding the maiden, she awoke and cried out in terror. "Who and what are you?" they asked.

"I am only a motherless child, driven from my home," she replied. "Have mercy on me, and take me with you!"

"Well," they said, "you may be useful to the cook, little Furball. We will take you with us; you can at least sweep up the ashes."

So they placed her on the wagon and took her to the King's castle. There they showed her a kennel under the steps, where no daylight ever came, and said: "Furball, here you may live and sleep." Then the Princess was sent into the kitchen to fetch the wood, draw the water, stir the fire, pluck the fowls, clean the vegetables, sweep the ashes, and do all the hard, dirty work.

Poor Furball lived for a long time as a servant of servants. She could not see how this life was ever to end, and how she was ever to be a king's daughter again. One day she heard that a festival was to take place in the castle, so she said to the cook: "May I go out for a little while to see the guests arrive? I promise you no one shall catch sight of little Furball."

"Go," the gruff old cook replied, "but in half an hour I shall want you to sweep up the ashes and put the kitchen in order."

Then Furball took her smoky oil lamp, ran into her kennel, threw off the fur coat, and washed the nut stains from her face and hands. Oh, but she was beautiful to see! She opened the nutshell, took out the dress that was golden as the sun, and put it on. It lighted up the kennel so that the lamp was ashamed and its smoky flame went out.

As soon as the Princess was dressed, she slipped around to the front of the castle and entered the great door as a guest. No one recognized her as Furball; the door-keepers thought she was a princess from some far country and they quickly told the King of her arrival. He hastened to meet her, bowed low to kiss her hand, and led her out to dance. While they danced he thought in his heart: "Never before have mine eyes seen any maiden so beautiful as this." And as they danced he slipped a gold ring on her finger.

As soon as the dance was over the Sun Princess curtesied to the King, smiled on him so brightly that his eyes were dazzled, and then vanished. The sentinel at the castle gate was called and questioned, but he had seen no one pass.

The Princess had run like a sunbeam to her kennel, taken off the gleaming dress, stained her face and hands, put on her fur coat, and was again Furball. When she entered the kitchen and reached for the broom to sweep up the ashes, the cook said: "Let that go until tomorrow; I want you to make some soup for the King. I am too busy. But do not let one of your hairs drop into the soup, or you will get nothing to eat for a week."

Furball made the King's soup as nicely as she could and toasted bread for it. When the soup was ready, she dropped the King's gold ring into the bowl.

After the ball was over, the King called for his supper, and declared he had never tasted better soup in his life. But when the dish was nearly empty, he saw, to his surprise, the gold ring at the bottom. He could not imagine how it came there, so he ordered the cook to appear before him.

The old cook was in a terrible fright when he heard the order. "You must have let a hair fall into the soup," he growled to Furball. "If you have, I shall give you a good beating and nothing to eat for a week."

As soon as the cook came shuffling into the banquet hall, the King demanded: "Who made this soup?"

"I made it, sire," faltered the frightened cook.

"That is not true," said the King. "This soup is much better than any soup of yours."

Then the cook had to confess that Furball made the soup.

"Go and send her to me," commanded the King.

As soon as ever little Furball appeared, all smutty from the kitchen, the King said to her: "Who are you, maiden, and of what mother born?"

"I am a poor, motherless child, a stranger in your kingdom, Sire," she replied.

"How came you in my castle?" he asked again.

"I serve the royal cook for shelter and for food."

"How came this ring in the soup?"

But Furball only looked at him and would not say a word.

When the King found he could learn nothing from her, he sent her away.

A few weeks later there was another festival, and Furball again begged leave from the cook to go and see the guests arrive at the great door of the palace.

"Go," he grunted, "but be sure you come back in a half hour and make for the King that soup he is so fond of."

She promised to obey, and ran quickly into her little kennel. There she washed off the walnut stains, took out of the nutshell her dress silvery as the moon, and put it on.

Again she appeared at the castle door like a foreign princess, and again the King came to meet her. He was so glad to see her that he would dance with no one else, and while they were dancing he pinned a tiny gold spinning wheel in her hair. But at the end of a half hour she disappeared so suddenly that the King could not imagine what had become of her. Like a moonbeam she slipped around the castle to her kennel, made herself again

43

the dark-faced, rough-coated little Furball, and went into the kitchen to make the King's soup.

When the soup was ready, she dropped the tiny gold spinning wheel into the bowl. The King ate the soup with great relish, but was amazed to find the gold spinning wheel in the bottom of the bowl. Again he sent for the cook and asked who made the soup, and again the cook had to confess that it was Furball. She was ordered to appear before the King, but when he asked her about the gold spinning wheel, Furball only looked at him and would not say a word.

At the King's third festival everything happened as before. The cook, when he told her she might go and see the guests arrive, growled: "Be back in time for the King's soup. I believe you are a witch. Your soup is good. The King says it is better than I can make; it can only be witchcraft that outdoes my cookery."

Furball did not stop to listen. She ran quickly to her little kennel, washed off the nut stains, and this time clad herself in the dress that glittered like the stars. When the King stepped forward quickly to receive her in the hall, as he had done twice before, he thought her the most beautiful maiden he had ever seen in all his life. While he held her hand in the dance, the King contrived to catch a gold hook into her sleeve.

He had given orders that the dancing should continue longer than usual, but the minute the music stopped Furball slipped her hand from the King's and was gone like a shooting star.

She was out of breath when she reached her kennel under the steps. She had stayed away longer than a half hour, she knew, and there was not time to take off her star dress. She threw her fur coat over it, and began to stain her face and hands. But she was in such a hurry that one finger remained white. When she reached the kitchen she made the King's soup and dropped into it the gold hook.

The King, when he found the small gold hook at the bottom of his bowl, sent at once for Furball, and as she entered the room he saw one white finger shining out from her little brown hand. He seized the hand and held her fast, while she struggled so to get free that the fur coat fell open and the glittering star dress came to view. The King drew off that coat of a thousand furs, and as he did so a flood of wonderful golden hair fell over the maiden's shoulders. She wiped the soot and stains from her face and hands, and stood before the King as the most glorious Princess on earth.

"You shall be my bride," said the young King, "for yours is the beauty of the sun and the moon and the stars."

Then the Princess told him all her story, and he loved her more than before. The next day the wedding took place, the cook made the best bridal soup he could, and the King and his beautiful Queen lived happy ever after.

DON'T BE AFRAID, BOYS

HOP O' MY THUMB

Once upon a time there was a poor woodcutter who had seven children, all boys. The eldest was ten, the youngest only seven. This youngest was a tiny chap—indeed, he was the smallest person ever seen. When he was born he was no bigger than his father's thumb, so everybody called him Hop o' my Thumb. Little Hop o' my Thumb almost never said a word, so nobody guessed how very much cleverer he was than any of his six brothers. For though he spoke only once in a while and said but little, he heard everything that went on.

The woodcutter and his wife at last became so poor they could no longer give their children enough to eat. One evening, when the boys were in bed, the husband said with a deep sigh:

"You see, my dear wife, we can find food for our children no longer. I cannot bear to see them die of hunger before my eyes, so I am going to take them into the forest tomorrow morning and leave them there. We will slip away from them, and they can never find their way back home."

"Oh!" cried the poor wife, "you surely cannot mean to leave your own children to perish!"

But her husband kept telling her to think how dreadful it would be to see the boys die of hunger before her very eyes, and at last the poor woman gave consent, and went weeping to bed.

Now Hop o' my Thumb had been awake all the time. When he heard his father talking so earnestly he slipped away from his brothers and hid behind his father's chair, to hear without being seen. When his father and mother stopped talking, he stole quietly back to bed and lay awake all night, trying to decide what he should do. In the morning he rose early and ran down to the stream. There he filled his pockets with smooth white pebbles and then hurried back home.

Soon they all set out for the forest, and Hop o' my Thumb said never a word about what he had heard. They went deep into the woods, and the woodcutter set to work chopping down trees, while the children gathered twigs for fagots. When the father and mother saw the boys were all busy, they slipped away quietly and went home by a bypath.

Soon the children found that they were alone, and began to cry at the top of their voices. Hop o' my Thumb let them cry for a while, but he smiled to himself. He knew how to lead them safely home! For had he not, as they came into the woods, dropped the white pebbles he had in his pocket all along the path? At last he said:

"Don't be afraid, boys. Father and mother have left us here by ourselves, but I can lead you back home again."

The brothers kept close to Hop o' my Thumb, who followed the pebbles, step by step, and so brought them to their father's house. They were afraid to go in, but they peeped through the window. Now it happened that just as the woodman and his wife reached home without their children, a great lord, galloping by, tossed them a piece of gold. The woodcutter sent his wife out to buy meat; and because she was so used to a large family, she bought enough for nine instead of two. When they had eaten all they wanted, she cried:

"Alas! where are our children? How they would feast on what we have left! Where are our children, our poor children?"

She said this so loud that the children, listening at the door, heard her, and cried out together, "Here we are, mother, here we are!"

The mother ran to let them in and kissed them all fondly: "How glad I am to see you, you little rogues!" she cried. "Are you not tired and hungry? Come in to dinner!"

The seven children sat down at the table and ate everything that was left. The parents looked on with delight,—a delight that lasted until the gold was all spent. Then they made up their minds they would have to lose their seven sons once more.

"This time," said the father, "we will take them much deeper into the forest, so they cannot find their way out."

They talked in whispers, but again Hop o' my Thumb heard all they said. Of course he thought he could do just what he did before; but when he slipped out of bed to get his white pebbles, he found that the door was double locked. Hop o' my Thumb did not know what to do. But when his mother gave him a piece of bread for breakfast, he made up his mind that this should take the place of the pebbles, and he put it into his pocket.

The father and mother took care, this time, to lead the children into the very thickest and darkest part of the forest. They left them there, and went home by a bypath as before. Hop o' my Thumb did not worry; he was sure he could find his way back by means of the crumbs he had scattered along the path. But to his surprise, not a morsel was left! The birds had come and eaten those crumbs all up!

The poor children were now in a terrible plight. The harder they tried to find their way out, the deeper they went into the forest. Night came on, and the wind began to howl. They thought it was the howling of wolves, and every moment they expected a wild beast to jump out and seize them.

Hop o' my Thumb climbed to the top of a tree and looked all about.

49

Far, far off, beyond the forest, he saw a little light, like a candle. When he came down he could not see it, but the children all started to walk in the direction in which he had seen the light. At last they reached the end of the forest, and the light shone out again. They hurried toward it, and finally reached a house from which the little light came. They knocked softly at the door and a big, pleasant-faced woman opened it, and asked them what they wanted.

"We are poor children," said Hop o' my Thumb. "We have lost our way in the woods. Please, please, let us come in and lie down until morning."

The woman, looking at their pleading childish faces, began to cry, and sobbed: "Oh, you poor children! What a place for you to come to! This is the house of an Ogre who eats little boys and girls."

"Deary me!" exclaimed Hop o' my Thumb, "what shall we do? If we go back to the woods, the wolves will surely eat us. We would rather stay here and be eaten by the Ogre. Maybe when he sees us he will be kind to us, if you coax him hard."

The Ogre's wife built no hope on her coaxing, but thought perhaps she could hide the boys from her husband till morning; so she let them in. She told them to warm themselves by the fire, before which there was a whole sheep roasting for the ogre's supper. While they were standing by the fire there came a loud knocking at the door. It was the Ogre! His wife hid the children under the bed and told them to lie still. Then she let her husband in.

"Is supper ready?" demanded the Ogre.

"Yes, all ready," replied his wife; and she put the sheep on the table before him. Pretty soon he began to sniff, and said: "I smell fresh meat."

"It must be the calf which has just been killed," answered his wife.

"I smell the flesh of a child," roared the Ogre. "There is something here that is hidden from the master of the house."

With these words, he jumped up from the table and went straight to the bed.

"Aha, wicked woman, so these are your tricks, are they?" he jeered,

reaching under the bed and feeling the children. "If you were n't so tough, old wife, I would eat you, too! But after all, this is lucky enough, for the brats will make a nice dish for the three Ogres, my special friends, who are to dine with me tomorrow."

His big, rough hands drew out the children one by one from under the bed. They fell on their knees, begging him to spare them. But this Ogre was the cruelest of all the Ogres, and he was already devouring them with his eyes. "Yes," he said to his wife, "they will be delicious morsels if you serve them up with a savory sauce."

Then he fetched a large knife and began to sharpen it on a whetstone, while the children shook with fear. Roughly snatching up one of the seven, he was just about to cut the boy to pieces, when his wife said to him:

"Why take the trouble to kill them tonight? Won't tomorrow be time enough?"

"Hold your tongue!" thundered the Ogre. "They will be tenderer for the keeping."

"But you have so much meat in the house already," answered his wife—— "a calf, two sheep, and half a pig."

"That's so," said the Ogre. "Give them a good supper to fatten them up a bit, and send them to bed."

So the kind woman set a good supper before them, but the poor children were too badly frightened to eat. As for the Ogre, he sat

down to his wine, chuckling over the thought of the treat in store for himself and his monster friends. And before long he stumbled off to bed.

Now this Ogre had seven daughters, all very young. They had fair complexions, because they ate raw meat, like their father; but they had small, round, gray eyes, hooked noses, wide mouths, and very long, sharp teeth set far apart. They were too young to have done a great deal of mischief, but they gave signs of being as cruel as the old Ogre himself, for they already delighted in biting little children. These young ogresses had gone to sleep early, all in one large bed. Each one had a little gold crown on her head. In their room was another bed, just the same size, and in this the Ogre's wife put the seven little boys, tying nightcaps under their chins. Of course, Hop o' my Thumb's bright eyes noticed that the young Ogresses all had gold crowns on their heads.

As he lay wide awake beside his sleeping brothers, Hop o' my Thumb began to be afraid the Ogre would feel sorry he had not killed them all that night. So about midnight he slid out of bed, took off the seven nightcaps, and crept over to the bed where the Ogre's daughters were sound asleep. He lifted off their gold crowns and tied the nightcaps on their heads instead; and then he put the crowns on himself and his brothers, and climbed back into bed.

"He will feel the crowns," thought Hop o' my Thumb, "and think we are his daughters."

Everything went just as he hoped. Soon after midnight the Ogre waked, sorry he had put off till the next day making ready for his feast. So he sprang out of bed and again whetted his knife till it was sharp enough to cut open his own hard heart.

"Now we'll see," he growled, "what these young rogues are about, and do the job at once!"

He stalked up to the room in which his daughters slept, and stole to the bed that held the boys. They were all fast asleep except Hop o' my Thumb. The Ogre passed his hand over the boys' heads one by one and felt the gold crowns.

"That would have been a pretty mistake!" he said. He went next to his daughters' bed and, feeling the nightcaps, grunted: "Here you are, you young rascals!" Then he killed all his daughters, one by one, without waking them at all, and went back to bed well satisfied with himself.

As soon as Hop o my Thumb heard the Ogre snoring, he woke his brothers and told them to put on their clothes and follow him. They

stole down to the garden and jumped from the wall into the road. They ran with all their might, almost all night without in the least knowing where they were going.

When the Ogre woke in the morning, he said to his wife: "Up, woman! Go and dress those tender lads I saw last night."

The Ogress was surprised at her husband's kindness, for she did not dream what he meant by *dressing* the boys. She went upstairs, and almost fainted when she saw her seven daughters all lying dead. The Ogre followed his wife to hurry her about the dinner, and was as amazed as she at what he saw.

"Oh, what have I done?" cried he. "They shall pay for this, the tricky runaways, before many minutes have passed!" Then the Ogre turned to his wife and cried: "Bring me my seven-league boots. I'll catch the little scamps!"

The Ogre set out with all speed, and strode about over the country looking for the boys. At last he turned into the road along which the poor children were hurrying toward their father's house. When they had almost reached it they saw the Ogre stalking from mountain top to

mountain top, and crossing rivers at one step. Hop o' my Thumb made his brothers crawl into a hollow in a rock, and then crept in himself. But you may be sure he kept his eye on the Ogre, to see what he would do next.

Now seven-league boots are very tiring, and the Ogre dropped down to rest on the very rock in which the children lay hidden. He fell asleep, and soon began to snore so loudly that the little fellows were as frightened as when the Ogre bent over them with the knife in his hand. But brave Hop o' my Thumb whispered to his brothers: "Run on home while he is asleep. I must stay here and see what he does."

The brothers did not need to be told twice, and were very soon at their father's house. In the meantime, Hop o' my Thumb went softly up to the Ogre, gently pulled off the seven-league boots, and drew them on his own legs. The boots seemed very large on the Ogre, but they were fairies, and could make themselves small enough to fit anyone. No sooner had Hop o' my Thumb put on the boots than he heard a friendly voice saying:

"Listen, Hop o' my Thumb! The boots you took from the Ogre are two fairies, my brother and I. We are pleased with your courage and your cleverness, and are ready to help you. Go to the Ogre's house, and when the Ogress opens the door, say:

'Ogress, Ogre cannot come;
Great key give to Hop o' my
Thumb.'"

Hop o' my Thumb repeated the two lines over and over that he might not forget them. When he was sure he had learned them by heart, he took two or three of his longest strides and reached the Ogre's door. He knocked loudly and the door was quickly opened by the Ogre's wife. When she saw Hop o' my Thumb she started back and would have shut the door; but Hop o' my Thumb cried out at once:

"Ogress, Ogre cannot come;
Great key give to Hop o' my
Thumb."

The Ogress, seeing her husband's boots, thought the Ogre must have sent Hop o' my Thumb on this errand. So she brought the great key and gave it to him, and even told him where to find the chest of money and jewels to which the key belonged. Hop o' my Thumb took a handful or two, enough to keep his father and mother and brothers in plenty for the rest of their lives, but left the chest still almost full for the Ogress, in return for her kindness to him and his brothers.

Of course, Hop o' my Thumb's family was very glad to see him.

The fame of his boots spread to the court, and the King sent for him, it is said, and employed him in many important affairs of the kingdom.

As for the wicked Ogre, he fell in his sleep from the corner of the rock from which Hop o' my Thumb and the other boys had escaped, and broke his wicked neck. When Hop o' my Thumb heard of his death, he told the King of all that the good-natured Ogress had done to save the lives of the seven lost children. The King was so pleased that he invited the Ogress to his court and bestowed on her the honorable title of Duchess of Draggletail.

LITTLE RED RIDING HOOD AND THE WOLF

LITTLE RED RIDING-HOOD

Once upon a time there was a little village girl who was as sweet as sugar and as good as bread. Her mother loved her very much, and her grandmother was even fonder of her. This kind grandmother had made her a pretty red cloak with a hood, in which the child looked so bright and gay that everyone called her Little Red Riding-Hood.

One day her mother made some cakes, and said to her: "Go, my child, and see how your grandmother is. I hear she has been ill. Take her one of these cakes and this little pot of butter."

So Little Red Riding-Hood set out at once to see her grandmother, who lived in another village.

As she walked through the woods she met a big wolf. He would have gobbled her up then and there, but some woodcutters were near by and he did not dare. But he did ask her where she was going. The little girl did not know it was dangerous to talk to a wolf, and so she said: "I am going to my grandmother with this cake and little pot of butter.

"Does she live far off?" asked the wolf.

"Oh, yes," answered Little Red Riding-Hood. "She lives beyond the mill you see way down there, at the first house in the village."

"All right," said the wolf. "I 'll go and visit her too. I will take this way, and you take that way, and we 'll see who gets there first."

And the wolf began to run as fast as he could along the shortest path, while Little Red Riding-Hood kept to the high road. She amused herself as she went along gathering nuts, chasing late butterflies, and making nosegays of the little autumn flowers.

Soon the wolf arrived at the grandmother's cottage, and knocked at the door — tap! tap!

"Who is there?"

"It is your own Little Red Riding-Hood," said the wolf, making his voice sound as much like Little Red Riding-Hood's as he could. "I have brought you a cake and a little pot of butter which mother has sent you."

The good old woman, who wasn't well and so was in bed, called out: "Pull the string, my dear, and the latch will fly up."

The wolf pulled the string and the door opened. He sprang upon the poor old grandmother and swallowed her all in one gulp, for it was more than three days since he had had a bite. He did not feel very well after that, but he shut the door, put on the grandmother's cap, and stretched himself out in the bed to wait for Little Red Riding-Hood. By-and-by Red Riding-Hood came knocking at the door—tap! tap!

"Who is there?"

At first Little Red Riding-Hood was frightened at the hoarse voice of the wolf. But she made up her mind her grandmother must have a cold.

"It is your own Little Red Riding-Hood," she answered. I have brought you a cake and a little pot of butter which mother has sent you."

Then the wolf called out, softening his voice as well as he could: "Pull the string, my dear, and the latch will fly up."

Little Red Riding-Hood pulled the string and the door opened.

When the wolf saw her come in, he hid under the bedclothes and said:

"Put the cake and the little pot of butter on the shelf, and come to bed with me."

And so Little Red Riding-Hood climbed into bed. She was very much surprised to see how strange her grandmother looked in her nightclothes and said:

"Grandmother, what great arms you have!" she cried.

"The better to hug you, my child!"

"Grandmother, what great ears you have!"

"The better to hear you, my child!"

"Grandmother, what great eyes you have!"

"The better to see you, my child!"

"Grandmother, what great teeth you have!"

"The better to eat you!"

With these words the wicked wolf fell upon poor Little Red Riding-Hood. And there the story ends. Nobody knows just what happened. Some say that the woodsmen came in just in time to save Little Red Riding-Hood, and when they cut the wolf open, there was grandmother whole and sound.

THE DANCING SHOES

There was once a King who had twelve daughters, each more beautiful than the one next younger, so that the eldest was most beautiful of all. They slept in one chamber where their beds stood side by side, and every night when they were well tucked in, the King locked and bolted the door. But when he unlocked the door in the morning he saw that their satin shoes had been danced to shreds, and no one could find out how that had come about, not even the royal schoolmaster, who was the wisest man in the world.

Then the King bade the heralds proclaim that he who could discover where and with whom the princesses danced at night, should choose one of them for his bride, but that whosoever dared to make the venture and failed to succeed within three nights should lose his liberty.

It was not long before a Prince came riding to the court and offered to make the trial. He was received and feasted with all honor, and in the evening was led into a room next to the great chamber where the princesses all slept. A bed was made ready for him beside a little window in the wall between the rooms, but he was warned not to sleep. He was to watch and see after this and undertook to solve the puzzle, but all fell asleep too soon and had to vanish.

Now it chanced that a poor Soldier who had been wounded and could serve his king and country no longer, found himself on the road that led to the city where the King lived. There he met an old dame, who asked him whither he was bound. "I hardly know myself," said he, and added in jest: "I had thought of trying my luck at finding out where the princesses dance their satin shoes to shreds."

"Try, brave Soldier," said the old dame, who was a fairy in disguise, "but mind you do not drink the wine that will be brought to you at night, even though it be offered by the hand of the eldest and most beautiful princess." With that she gave him a short green cloak embroidered with fern seed, and said: "When you wear this, you will be invisible, but you must be careful to tread as silently as a shadow." So the Soldier took heart, went to the King, and announced himself as a suitor. He was honored for his wounds and feasted as well as the princes.

That evening at bedtime he was led into the antechamber where the eldest princess graciously offered him a goblet of wine through the

where they went and danced, just as their nurse used to watch them through the window that, though small, was large enough to let her go in to them when they were ill or naughty.

But the eyelids of the Prince grew heavy with sleep, for he had traveled far and feasted well. Soon he sank into a deep slumber, and when he awoke in the morning, beside each empty bed stood a pair of white satin shoes with the soles danced into holes. On the second and third nights it happened just as before, and the poor Prince was given over to the court wizard, who had only to wave his ivory wand over a man and at once that man vanished like a puff of smoke. Other princes came

THE PRINCESS OFFERED THE PRINCE A GOBLET OF WINE

youngest said: "I know not how it is. You are all gay, but I feel frightened; some danger is whispering to my heart."

"Little goose, thou art ever frightened," said the eldest. "I, for one, never felt so glad before. Hast thou forgotten how many kings' sons have already tried in vain? What harm can come to us from this poor Soldier, so tired that he hardly needed the wine with its juice of sleepy poppy?"

When they were all dressed for the ball, each of the twelve princesses slipped her head through the little window for a look at the Soldier. He seemed fast asleep, so they felt quite secure. The eldest went to her bed and tapped it; it instantly sank through the floor, and one princess after the other sprang through the opening, the eldest going first.

The Soldier, who had watched everything from under his eyelashes, did not tarry longer, but threw on the fern-seed cloak, slipped through the window, and went down last. The twelve princesses were descending by a marble stair into the heart of the earth. Halfway down the Soldier trod on the long silk train of the youngest; she was terrified and cried out: "What is that? Some one is pulling at my dress."

"Don't be so foolish!" called back the eldest. "Did no train ever catch

window. He took the goblet with all courtesy from her hand, but he had tied a sponge under his chin, and so let the wine run down into it without drinking a drop. Then he fell upon his bed beside the little window and after a few minutes began to snore like a trumpet. The twelve princesses in the next room laughed to hear him, but the eldest said: "It is a pity that so brave a Soldier must vanish."

Meanwhile they were all opening cupboards, wardrobes, and presses, bringing out their daintiest dresses, curling their hair before the mirrors, skipping about, and rejoicing at the prospect of the dance. Only the on a stair before?" Then they went farther and farther down into strange spaces lit only by jewels, till at last they stood in a wonderful avenue of trees, all whose leaves were of silver that shone and glittered like moonlight.

The Soldier thought: "I must carry some token away with me," and broke off a twig from one of those silver branches. As he did so the tree cracked with a loud report, so that he thought for a moment he was back in the wars.

The youngest princess cried out again: "All is not well. Did you hear that sound of warning?"

But the eldest said: "Tush! my heart was never so light. Those are triumphal salutes because we shall soon have set our princes free from enchantment."

Next they came to an avenue where the leaves were all of gold, and then to a third where they were all of dazzling diamonds. The Soldier broke off a twig from a gold branch and another from a diamond branch, and each time there was such a loud crack that the youngest princess cried out in terror, but the eldest laughed at her and still said that these reports were royal salutes.

They went on and on and on until they came to a great lake, like one huge melted sapphire. Here were moored twelve little boats, and in each sat a joyous prince. They were waiting for the twelve princesses, and each took one of them into his boat. Last of all the Soldier, still invisible in his fern-seed cloak, seated himself by the youngest. Soon her prince said: "I can't tell why the boat is so heavy to-night; I must row with all my strength if we are to get across."

"It is all strange to-night," said the youngest princess. "It may be my heart that weighs so heavy in the boat."

On the further side of the lake stood a splendid, brilliantly lighted castle, whence sounded the merry music of elfin horns and bugles. The princes moored their boats, led their ladies into the castle, and there each prince danced with the princess he loved; but the Soldier, all unseen, danced with the eldest princess. When the youngest, whom he liked to tease, had a cup of wine in her hand, he drank it up, so that the cup was empty when she put it to her lips. She was alarmed at the loss of her wine, but the eldest princess danced more madly than ever before.

The ball went on until the cocks began to crow far above their heads on earth. All the white satin shoes were in holes by that time and the dance-music ceased. The princes rowed their ladies back again across the lake, and this time the Soldier seated himself close by the eldest princess. On the shore the royal runaways bade farewell to their princes, promising to return the following night and give them another recess from their enchantment. At sight of the marble stair the Soldier ran on ahead, treading softly as a shadow.

When the twelve princesses were back in their room, he was already snoring so loud that they laughed and said: "No danger for us from this sleepyhead of a soldier." They took off their ball-dresses, laid them away, and set the worn-out shoes beside the beds, then lay down, and were soon lost in happy dreams.

Next morning the Soldier resolved to hold his peace, that he might go with them to their wonderful world again. Everything came to pass just as it had the night before. The twelve princesses danced until their shoes were worn to shreds. The second time he carried an emerald fern away with him as a token and the third time a ruby rose.

So on the fourth morning, when the hour had come for his answer, he took the three twigs, the fern, and the rose, and stood in the throne room before the King, while the twelve princesses crowded behind the door and listened for what he was going to say. When the King put the question: "Where do my twelve daughters dance their shoes to shreds every night?" he answered: "In an underground castle with twelve enchanted princes." Then he related what he had seen and where he had gone, and brought out the tokens.

The King had the heralds call in a loud voice for his daughters, who came out quickly from behind the door. Their father asked them whether the Soldier had told the truth, and like kings' daughters they held up their heads and confessed all. Thereupon the King asked the Soldier which princess he would have as his bride. The youngest shrank away in terror, but he said: "Sire, the most beautiful—the eldest."

So the marriage was celebrated on that very day, and the bewitched princes of the underground castle were set free from their enchantment and danced at the wedding— all except the prince who had been used to dance with the eldest princess. He chose to stay down in the heart of the earth and reign as king in the splendid castle by the sapphire lake.

BEAUTY AND THE BEAST

BEAUTY AND THE BEAST

Once upon a time, there was a merchant who was very, very rich. This merchant had three boys and three girls. The three daughters were all pretty, but the youngest was the prettiest of all. Indeed, she was so beautiful that everyone, during her childhood, called her Little Beauty. When she grew up the name clung to her and this made her sisters jealous.

Now Beauty was not only prettier than her sisters, but she was better tempered, too, and kind and good to all. The elder sisters were proud and haughty and selfish, and would have nothing to do with anyone who was not rich and grand.

One evening the merchant came home tired and sad. He had suddenly lost his huge fortune. He no longer had plenty of money, and their beautiful home, with its lovely lawns, trees and flowers, must be sold. All that was left was a little cottage in the country, and the family must move out there to live. With the tears running down his cheeks the merchant said to his sons and daughters:

"My children, we must go and live in the cottage and we shall have to work hard to earn our living."

The big sisters did not want to go at all, but Beauty was glad, for she loved the country, and liked nothing better than to take long walks through the woods and fields.

When the family was settled in the cottage, the merchant and his three sons worked hard in the fields from sunrise to sunset, and managed to make enough money on which to live. Beauty was a great help to her father. She rose at four o'clock, put the house in order, and got breakfast for the whole family. It was hard at first, for she was not used to working like a servant, but it grew easier and easier, and Beauty grew healthier and rosier. She became a fine little housekeeper, a fine little cook, and a fine little laundress. When she had finished her work, she would amuse herself with reading, or playing on the harpsichord, or spinning the golden flax, singing as she spun.

Her sisters did not know what to do to pass the time. They did not get up until ten o'clock. Then they strolled about, wailing over the loss of their carriage and their fine clothes. And they despised poor Beauty because she was not as miserable as they were.

"Since you are so kind as to think of me, dear father," answered Beauty, "I should like to have you bring me a rose, for we have none in our garden."

It was not that Beauty cared so much for a rose, but she did not want it to look as if she were trying to be better than her sisters, who would have said she refused only to be praised.

The father set out on his journey, but when he reached the port he had to go to law about the cargo. After a great deal of trouble he started back as poor as when he left home.

He was within thirty miles of his home, and was thinking of how happy he would be to see his children again. But his road lay through a thick forest, and in a blinding storm he lost his way. All at once, down a long avenue of trees, he saw a golden gleam which seemed to be at a great distance. He rode toward it and found that it shone from a splendid palace brightly lighted from top to bottom. Not a soul was to be seen in any of the outer yards.

The stable door stood open, and the merchant's horse, half-starved, walked in and helped himself to a plentiful meal of oats and hay. Leaving his horse in the stable, the

The family had been living in the cottage about a year when one morning a letter came to the merchant. This letter told him that one of his richest ships, which he had thought lost, had come at last to port.

The two elder sisters were wild with joy. When their father set out for the port they begged he would bring back to them new gowns, caps, rings, and all sorts of trinkets. Beauty asked for nothing, for she thought that all the ship's cargo would scarcely buy what her sisters had asked for.

"Don't you want me to bring you anything, Beauty?" asked her father.

merchant went into the house. Still he found no one. But in a large room he found a cheerful fire and a table spread with the finest food. The table was set for one.

As the rain and snow had wet him to the skin, he went and stood before the fire.

"Surely," he said to himself, "the master of the house or his servants will pardon the liberty I am taking. Of course some one will come before long."

He waited and waited, but no one came. When the clock struck eleven, he decided he could endure his hunger no longer. So he helped himself to a chicken, which he ate to the bones, all the time trembling with fear. Now that he no longer felt hungry, he took courage and began to look about him. He passed through one beautifully furnished room after another, and finally came to a chamber in which there was an inviting couch. It was past midnight and he was very tired, so he shut the door and went to bed.

It was ten o'clock the next morning when he waked. And what was his astonishment to see beside his bed a handsome new suit of clothes, instead of his own, which were quite worn out!

"Surely," he said to himself, "this palace belongs to a good fairy, who

has taken pity on me and cared for me in my trouble."

He looked out of the window and saw no snow, but a lovely flower garden. He returned to the room where he had eaten the night before and there he found a little table spread with fruit and eggs, a plate of buttered toast, and a pot of fragrant hot coffee.

"Thank you, good fairy," he said aloud, "for your kind care of me."

After breakfast he started toward the stable to look after his horse. As he passed through the rose garden he remembered what Beauty had asked for, and he picked a spray of roses to carry home. As he was picking them he heard a terrible noise, and saw such a frightful beast coming toward him that he almost fainted with fear.

"Ungrateful man!" roared the Beast. "I saved your life by receiving you in my palace, and in return you steal my roses, which I love more than anything else in the world. You shall pay for this with your life."

The merchant threw himself on his knees, crying:

"My lord, forgive me! I did not mean to offend you. I picked only this one spray for my youngest daughter who had asked me to bring her a rose."

"I am not a lord," replied the monster, "but a beast. I do not like sweet words, so do not think you can soften me with flattery. You say you have daughters. I will pardon you if one of them will come and die in your place. Do not try to argue with me, but go; and swear to me that if your daughters refuse, you will come back in three months."

The merchant did not intend for a moment to let one of his daughters die for him. But he thought that if he pretended to do what the

Beast asked he would at least see his children again. So he promised, and the Beast told him he might set off as soon as he pleased.

"But," added the Beast, "I don't want you to go empty-handed. Go back to the room in which you slept. There you will find an empty chest which you may fill with whatever you like best. I will send it to your house."

The Beast then went away, and the merchant said to himself:

"If I must die, I shall at least be able to leave something for my children."

He went back to the room in which he had slept. There he found a great quantity of gold pieces and, after slipping five into his purse, he filled the chest to the very brim with them. Then he mounted his horse and set out for home. The horse found his way through the forest, and in a few hours the merchant reached his cottage. All six children gathered around him. After giving to each of the others a gold piece, he handed to Beauty the spray of roses, saying:

"Take it, Beauty; little do you think what it has cost your poor father."

Then he told them all that had happened in the Beast's palace. The two elder sisters began to weep, and

to blame Beauty, who did not shed a tear.

"See," said they, "what the pride of the little wretch has done! Why did she not ask for fine things as we did? But no, she must do something different! And now she is causing her father's death, yet she does not shed a tear!"

"Why should I weep?" said Beauty. "My father will not die. I shall in his stead give myself up to the Beast."

"No, no, sister!" cried the three brothers. "You shall not die. We will go and find this monster, and he or we will perish."

"You can never kill him," said the merchant. "You have no idea how powerful he is. I cannot thank Beauty enough for her love, but I will not let her die for me."

"You shall never go to the palace without me," cried Beauty. "You cannot prevent my following you."

The merchant was so unhappy at the thought of losing Beauty that he never thought of the chest of gold. But when he went to his room at night, he found it standing by his bedside. He said nothing to his elder daughters about his treasure, for he knew they would want it for dowries to win them husbands, but he told Beauty the secret.

When the three months had passed, the merchant and Beauty set out for the palace of the Beast. The two sisters rubbed their eyes with an onion to make believe they shed a great many tears, but the merchant and his sons really wept. Beauty did not cry, for she thought this would only make the others more unhappy.

The horse took the right road of his own accord and when they reached the palace, went at once to the stable. Hand in hand, the merchant and Beauty entered the house, and there they found a table set for two, with the most delicious things to eat. After supper they heard a roar like thunder; and the poor merchant wept as he told Beauty good-by, for she had persuaded him, for the sake of his other children, to leave her there alone.

Beauty, when she saw the terrible Beast, all claws and bristles, trembled a little, but she tried to be as brave as she could. The monster asked her if she had come of her own free will.

"Y-e-s," she answered, trembling.

"You are a good girl," growled the Beast, "and I thank you. As for you," he said to the father, who, forgetting his promise had rushed back to protect his child, "you are to leave this place to-morrow morning. Take care that you never find your way here again. Good-night, Beauty!"

"Good-night, Beast!" she answered in her sweet-toned voice, and the monster shuffled away.

"O my child," groaned the merchant, "I cannot leave you to such a fate. Go home and let me stay."

"No," replied Beauty. "What would become of the other children without you? You must go home to-morrow morning."

They now wished each other a sorrowful good-night and went to bed. In the morning the merchant kissed Beauty good-by and rode sadly toward home. When he was out of sight Beauty sat down and cried. But she was really a brave girl and soon dried her tears and began to explore the palace. What was her surprise at coming to a doorway over which was written "Beauty's room!" She opened the door, and her eyes were dazzled by the splendor of the chamber. But she was most pleased with the many books, the harpsichord, and the music.

"Does the Beast want me to be happy?" she wondered. "Surely he would not have done all this for me if I had only one day to live."

She opened a book, in which was written in letters of gold:

"You may wish for anything, you may order anything. You are queen and mistress here."

"Alas!" thought Beauty, "there is nothing I want so much as to see my poor father, and to know what he is doing now."

Just then she glanced at a large looking-glass, and lo and behold! she saw her home, and her father riding up to the cottage. Her sisters had come out to meet him and they were trying to look sorry, but they could not hide their joy because Beauty had not come back. Beauty saw the picture for only a moment, but she began to think that the Beast might mean to be kind to her. Surely she need not be afraid of him!

At noon she found dinner served, and as she ate she heard the sweetest music, though she saw no one. That evening Beauty was just sitting down to the supper table when she heard the shuffle of great shaggy paws, and she could not help trembling with terror.

"Beauty," growled the Beast, standing up pleadingly on his hind legs, "will you give me the pleasure of seeing you sup?"

"That is as you wish," answered Beauty.

"Tell me, Beauty," asked the Beast, "do you think I am very, very ugly?"

"Yes, Beast," said Beauty, "I cannot tell a lie. But I think you are very good."

Beauty ate with an excellent appetite, and the Beast was so humble and polite she had nearly got the better of her fear of him when he asked:

"Beauty, will you marry me?"

She was afraid of making the monster angry if she refused, but said bravely:

"No, Beast."

The Beast sighed so deeply that he shook the palace, and sadly said: "Good-night, Beauty!" Then he left her, and Beauty began to feel sorry for him.

"Alas!" she said, "what a pity he is so frightful, since he is so good."

Beauty lived three months in the palace very contentedly. The Beast visited her every evening. Beauty grew used to his ugliness, and every evening she saw more clearly how good he was. But there was one thing that made her unhappy. Every evening before he left her the Beast asked her to marry him. And when, every evening, she said no, his sighs made the palace rock as if in a high wind. At last one night the Beast said to her:

"If you will not marry me, at least promise me, Beauty, that you will never leave me."

"No," said Beauty, weeping, "I will never cause your death. I promise to come back in a week."

"You shall find yourself with your father to-morrow morning," answered the Beast. "But remember your promise. When you wish to come back, just put your ring on a table when you go to bed. Good-by, dear Beauty."

When Beauty awoke in the morning she found herself at home in her father's cottage. Her father was so happy to see Beauty that he almost died of joy. He sent word of her return to the sisters, who came hurrying over with their husbands

Now Beauty, that very day, had seen in her looking-glass that her father had fallen sick of grief, so she said:

"I would willingly promise never to leave you, but I shall die if I cannot go and see my dear father. He is ill and poor. My sisters have found that chest of gold you gave my father, have divided it for dowries and are married, my brothers are away in the army, and he is alone. Oh, please, good Beast, do not refuse me!"

"I would rather die myself, dear Beauty," replied the Beast, "than to make you unhappy. You may go to your father, and your poor Beast shall die of grief."

to pay her a visit. The husband of the eldest sister was extremely handsome; but he was so vain of his good looks that he thought of nothing else from morning till night. The second sister had married a very clever man, but the only use he made of his cleverness was to torment his friends and his wife.

The two sisters were more jealous than ever when they saw Beauty dressed like a princess and looking so very beautiful. They made a plan to end her happiness.

"Let us," said the elder, "try to keep her here after her week's leave is over. The Beast will surely be so angry that he will eat her up in a moment."

So when the week was ended, the two sisters began to tear their hair, and shed so many tears at the thought of Beauty's leaving them that she consented to stay a few days longer. But she could not help feeling sorry for the poor Beast, who was being made so unhappy.

The tenth night that Beauty was in her father's home she dreamed she was strolling in the garden of the palace. On the grass lay the Beast, almost dead. Beauty awoke and burst into tears.

"How wicked I am," she said, "to be so ungrateful to my kind Beast!"

She laid her ring on the table and soon fell asleep again. In the morning she found herself in the Beast's palace. All day she wished for the supper hour, that the Beast might come. She had never passed so long a day. At length the clock struck seven, but no Beast came. Beauty ran from room to room of the palace, calling him, but no one answered. At last she remembered her dream, and ran toward the grass plot on which she had dreamed she saw him. There lay the poor Beast on the grass.

Beauty threw herself on the shaggy body, and finding that his heart was still beating, she ran quickly for water and threw it on his face. The Beast quickly opened his eyes and said:

"You forgot your promise to me, dear Beauty. And my grief was so great that I tried to starve myself to death. Now, Beauty, I shall die happy, for I have seen you once more."

"No, dear Beast," cried Beauty, "you shall not die. You must live to be my husband. I thought I felt only gratitude, but now I know I love you."

As soon as Beauty had said these words, the palace and the garden suddenly blazed with light. Music sounded, fireworks shone. Beauty turned to look at her dear Beast, but suddenly no Beast was to be seen in the garden. Instead, the very handsomest prince that was ever seen knelt at Beauty's feet and thanked her for having broken his enchantment.

"But where is my dear Beast?" asked Beauty.

"You see him, Beauty, at your feet," answered the Prince. "A wicked fairy had given me the form of a beast, and declared that I must keep it until a beautiful girl should love me and consent to marry me."

Beauty went with the Prince to the palace, where, to her delight, she found her dear father and all her family. Together the happy company traveled to the young Prince's dominions, and there the Prince was received with great joy by his subjects, who had mourned him as lost. The Prince married Beauty, and together they reigned happily for a long, long time.

CINDERELLA AND HER GODMOTHER

CINDERELLA OR THE LITTLE GLASS SLIPPER

Once upon a time there was a little girl whose dear mother died, and whose father married for his second wife the proudest and unkindest woman that ever was seen. She had two daughters who were exactly like her in every way. The little girl, on the other hand, was all sweetness and goodness, for she took after her mother, who had been the best woman in the world.

No sooner was the wedding over than the new wife began to show her bad temper. She could not bear the gentleness of the little girl because it made the sharp voices and selfish ways of her own daughters seem more hateful, and she put her to doing the hardest work in the house. She made her wash the dishes and scrub the stairs and clean up the rooms till the house was neat enough for the Queen of the Cats, but still the child, at the end of her day's toil, had only a scolding for supper.

At night the poor little girl slept alone on a straw sack in the attic, while her sisters slept in fine rooms on soft beds of the very latest fashion, and had looking glasses so tall that they could see themselves from top to toe. But she bore it all cheerfully, never complaining to her father, who had troubles enough of his own.

When her work was done she used to cuddle down in the chimney corner in the ashes and cinders to keep warm. For this reason she was called Ash-girl; but the younger sister, who was not quite so rude as the elder, called her Cinderella. Now in spite of Cinderella's ragged clothes, she was a hundred times prettier than her sisters in their elegant dresses.

It happened one day that the King's son gave a ball and invited to it all the grand folk. Of course Cinderella's sisters were invited, because with their airs and graces they were very fine ladies indeed.

They were wild with delight. They busied themselves choosing what gowns they should wear and deciding what manner of headdress would become them most. But it meant only more work for Cinderella, because it was she who had to iron her sisters' linen and plait their ruffles and flounces. All day long, the sisters talked of nothing but of how they were going to dress.

"I," said the elder, "shall wear my red velvet robe, with my wonderful lace trimming."

"I," said the younger, "shall wear my ordinary dropskirt, but I shall drape over it my gold-brocaded train; and I shall put on my emeralds. I shall not look plain, I can tell you that!"

At last they called in Cinderella to ask her advice, for they knew she had the best of taste. She offered to dress their hair for them, and they were glad enough to have her do it.

While she was dressing their hair they said to her:

"Cinderella, don't you wish you might go to the ball?"

"You are only making fun of me," said poor Cinderella. "Ash-girls don't go to balls at the palace, as you very well know."

"Right you are!" they exclaimed. "How people would laugh to see a sooty ash-girl at the ball!"

Any one but Cinderella would have put their hair up all crooked, but Cinderella, who was as good as she was pretty, only tried to make her sisters look as well as she possibly could. They had gone almost two days without eating, so excited were they about going to the ball, but in spite of that, they broke about a dozen corset strings trying to make themselves look slender, and they spent hours and hours before their tall mirrors.

At last the happy evening arrived. The two sisters set out for the ball, and Cinderella watched them as far as her eyes could see. When their carriage had rolled out of sight, she burst into tears. Suddenly her godmother, a little old lady leaning on an ivory staff, stood before her and asked what the trouble was.

"I want—I want," sobbed poor Cinderella, but the tears came so fast she could say nothing more.

Her godmother, who was a fairy, knew quite well what she wanted. "You wish you might go to the ball. Is it not so?"

"Yes," said Cinderella, with a deep sigh.

"Well, then," said her godmother, "be a good girl and I will see that you go to the ball. Run out into the garden and bring me a pumpkin."

Cinderella did not see what on earth a pumpkin could have to do with her going to the ball, but she ran quickly, chose the biggest and finest pumpkin on the vines, and carried it to her godmother.

Her godmother scooped it out so that nothing but the rind was left. She touched it lightly with her ivory staff, and the pumpkin was changed into a splendid gilded coach.

Then she went and looked into the mouse trap, where she found six live mice. She told Cinderella to lift the door of the trap just a little, and as each mouse ran out she tapped it lightly with her staff, and at once it became a spirited steed. Altogether, they soon had a fine turnout of six prancing mouse-gray horses in bright, jingling harness.

But what to do for a coachman?

"I will go and see if there are not some rats in the rat trap," cried Cinderella. "We might make a coachman out of one of them!"

"Good!" said her godmother. "Run and see."

So Cinderella brought the rat trap. In it there were three big rats. The fairy chose the plumpest one with the longest whiskers, and changed him into a jolly fat coachman with the finest sweeping mustaches you ever saw.

Then the godmother said:

"Go into the garden and bring me the six lizards you will find behind the watering pot."

Cinderella had no sooner brought the lizards than her godmother changed them into six footmen. They jumped up behind the coach and sat there as stiff and straight in their gold-braided uniforms as if they had done nothing else all their lives. Then the fairy said:

"Now you have all you need to take you to the ball. Are you not happy?"

"Yes," faltered Cinderella, "but how can I go in these ragged clothes?"

The godmother just touched her with her staff, which was really a fairy wand, and in a moment the rags were changed to a dress of gold and silver tissue embroidered with precious stones. And on Cinderella's feet was a pair of glass slippers, the most dainty and graceful little slippers in this world.

Cinderella climbed into her gilded coach, the chubby coachman cracked his whip, but before the fiery horses had sprung forward, her godmother said to her:

"Remember, my child, you must not stay one minute after midnight. For if you do, your coach will change back to a pumpkin, your horses will be mice, your coachman a rat, your footmen lizards, and your beautiful gown the same old clothes you wore before."

Cinderella promised that she would surely leave the ball before midnight, and away she drove, almost beside herself with joy. The King's son, when he heard that a beautiful Princess whom no one knew, had come, ran down the steps to meet her. He gave her his hand as she alighted from the carriage, and led her into the ballroom.

At once everyone became silent. The dancing stopped; the musicians left off playing. No one could do anything but look at this radiant Princess whom no one knew. On all sides was heard the whisper:

"Oh, how beautiful she is!"

Even the old King could do nothing but gaze at her, and he whispered very low to the Queen:

"My dear, not since you were a young girl have I seen any one so charming!"

All the ladies of the court were busy staring at Cinderella's robe, hoping they might be able to copy it the very next day. But where could they find such glorious stuff, and where could they find sewing women clever enough to follow so rare a pattern?

The young Prince led Cinderella to the seat of honor, and begged for the next dance. She danced so gracefully that everyone admired her more than ever. When supper was served, the young Prince ate nothing, because he could not take his eyes off Cinderella, who seated herself near her sisters and shared with them the fruit and sweetmeats which the Prince gave her. They were very much surprised at such kindness from this great and gracious lady. As she was still talking with them the clock struck three quarters after eleven, and Cinderella at once excused herself, courtesied to the Prince, and hurried away.

As soon as she reached home she ran to find her godmother and thanked her again and again.

"And, oh, godmother," she coaxed, "may I not go once more tomorrow night? Because the King's son begged me to come."

But before her godmother could make reply her sisters knocked at the door. The fairy godmother disappeared and Cinderella ran to let them in.

"Oh, how long you have been!" cried Cinderella, rubbing her eyes and yawning as if she had just waked.

If Cinderella was sleepy now, you may be sure she had been far from sleepy all the evening!

"If you had been at the ball," said one of her sisters, "you would not have been yawning! There was the most beautiful and the most gracious Princess there that has ever been seen! She showed us a thousand attentions. She shared with us the fruit and sweetmeats which the King's son bestowed upon her."

Cinderella could scarcely conceal her mirth as she asked the name of the Princess.

"We don't know," said her sisters. "The King's son himself would give anything in the world to find out who she is."

Cinderella sighed and said:

"She surely must have been lovely! Oh, how lucky you were to see her! How I wish I could see her, too! Oh, my Lady Javotte, please lend me that yellow frock you wear every day, so that I may go to the ball and look on the Princess!"

"I see myself doing it!" sneered Lady Javotte. "Wouldn't I be silly to lend my nice frock to a dirty little ash-girl!"

Cinderella did not mind, for she would not have known what to do with the yellow dress if Lady Javotte had really lent it to her.

The next night the sisters went to the ball. Cinderella went, too, but she was clad even more charmingly than on the night before. The Prince stayed close beside her, and never stopped whispering love words into her ear. Cinderella was so happy she quite forgot what her godmother had told her. When the first stroke of midnight sounded, she was sure it could not be later than eleven. But when she found it was really twelve, she sprang up and ran out of the ballroom like a startled deer.

The Prince hurried after her, but he could not overtake those flying feet. As she ran, Cinderella dropped one of her glass slippers, and this the prince picked up most carefully.

Cinderella reached home all out of breath, without coach, without footmen, in the same sooty, ragged clothes she wore every day. All she had left of her finery was one little glass slipper.

The Prince asked the guards at the palace door if they had not

seen the Princess run out. No, the guards said, they had seen only a young girl, poorly dressed, and more like a peasant than a princess.

When the two sisters returned from the ball Cinderella asked if the beautiful · lady had been there.

"Yes," they said. "But as the clock struck twelve she ran away so fast that she dropped one of her little glass slippers. The King's son found it, and all the rest of the evening he did nothing but look at it. It is plain to be seen he is much in love with its owner, and will never rest until he has found the Princess to whom it belongs."

What they said was true. A few days later the Prince's messenger rode through the streets and blew a great blast on his long silver trumpet. Then he cried in a loud voice that the King's son would marry the maiden who could wear the glass slipper.

The slipper was tried first on the princesses, then on the duchesses and court ladies, but it fitted no one. Finally it was carried to Cinderella's home, and tried on the two sisters. Each did her best to squeeze her foot into it, but it was far too small.

Cinderella, who had been watching them, and who knew her slipper, said with a smile:

"What if I were to try?"

Her sisters began to jeer at her, but the King's herald turned and looked at her closely. He saw even through the soot that she was beautiful, and declared it was only right that she, too, should try on the slipper. She sat down, he knelt and held the little slipper to her foot, and it fitted her like wax.

The sisters gasped with amazement, but they were even more surprised when Cinderella took the other slipper from her pocket and slipped it on her other foot. No sooner had she done this than her godmother appeared. She touched Cinderella with her wand, and there stood the Princess who had gone to the ball, but even more richly dressed than before. When the two sisters saw that it was really Cinderella who stood before them, they fell on their knees and begged her to forgive them. She lifted them up, kissed them, forgave them, and begged them to love her always.

She was led to the Prince, who thought her lovelier than ever, and married her as soon as the priest could find the wedding service in the prayer book. And then because Cinderella was as good as she was pretty, she took her sisters with her to the palace, and there, after their tempers and manners had improved, she married them to two fine gentlemen of the court.

RUMPEL-STILT-SKIN

Once upon a time there lived a poor miller who had a very beautiful daughter. He was so proud of her beauty and cleverness he boasted the livelong day about her. One day he even dared tell the King his daughter could spin gold out of straw. Now the King loved gold far better than anything else in his kingdom, and when he heard the miller's boast, he commanded the maiden to be brought before him.

She was so beautiful he almost forgot his purpose, but soon he led the maiden to a large room about half full of straw, gave her a spinning wheel and said: "If all this straw is not spun into gold by morning, you shall die." Then he went out, locked the door with a huge key, and left her alone.

The poor girl sat down in a corner of the room and began to cry, for she knew no more than the King himself about spinning straw into gold. All of a sudden the door opened just a crack and a comical little man squeezed in.

"Good day, miller's daughter," he said. "What are you crying about?"

"Ah me!" she sobbed, "I must die on the morrow, for I know not how to spin this straw into gold."

"What will you give me if I do it for you?" asked the little man.

"This necklace I am wearing," replied the maiden.

The little man agreed and, sitting down at the wheel, sent it round right merrily, and presently the heap of straw was gone and the gold all spun. Then he twisted the necklace twice about his waist, stuck his little sword into this new belt of his and strutted away, leaving his cap for her breakfast.

When the King came next morning, he was very much pleased but far from satisfied. The more gold he had, the more he wanted. So he led the girl to a still larger room two thirds full of straw, and ordered her on peril of her life to spin it all into gold before sunrise. Again she began to cry and again the little man slipped through the crack of the door and said: "What will you give me, miller's daughter, to spin your straw to-night?"

"This ring on my finger," she replied.

So the droll little man set the wheel whirring again, twice as fast as before, and by daylight all was finished. Then he put on the ring as a bracelet, capered for pride and was gone, leaving his jacket for her breakfast.

The King came at dawn and was delighted to see the store of gold, yet his greedy heart was not satisfied. He took the miller's daughter into a vast chamber packed to the ceiling with straw except where the spinning wheel stood, and said: "Let all this straw be spun into gold to-night and you shall be my queen."

As soon as she was alone, in squeezed the queer little man again and said: "And what shall I have this third time for my labor?"

"I have nothing more," sighed she.

"Then you must promise to give me your first child after you become queen," said the little man.

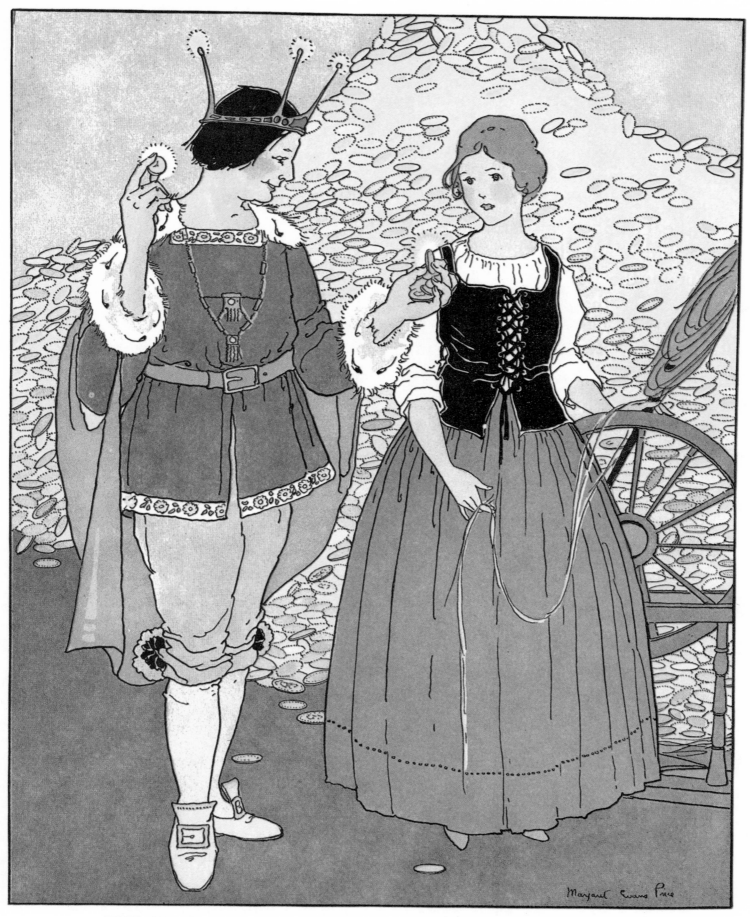

THE KING WAS DELIGHTED TO SEE THE STORE OF GOLD

"But what may not happen before then?" thought the maiden, and as she knew no other way out of her trouble, she promised to do what he asked.

That night he sang as he spun and the wheel whirred thrice as fast as before, so that when the sun shone into the chamber, all the straw was gold. The comical little man had to go out by the window, for the King came earlier than ever, thinking not only of the gold but of the beauty of the miller's daughter, whom he made his queen.

At the birth of her first child the Queen was overjoyed. She had

quite forgotten the queer little man, when one day he slipped into her chamber and said: "Where is the child you promised me?"

Then she was in sore distress. In vain she offered him all the treasures of the kingdom. But as the queer little man tucked the royal baby snugly under his arm, she gave such a cry that his odd little heart, like a dry currant, softened and he said: "I will give you three days to guess my name. If you can do it, you may keep the child." And he dropped the baby with a bump back into the cradle.

The Queen lay awake the night long, thinking of all the names she had ever heard. The next day when the little man came, she began with the names of the three kings of the East, Caspar, Melchior, Balthazar, and asked him the names of all the kings and princes that had lived since. But to all of them he gleefully said:

"Ho, ho! No, no, my Royal Dame!
That's not my name; that's not my name."

The next day she sent messengers throughout the kingdom to collect all the curious names of poor folk. And when the little man skipped in, she began with: "Cow-ribs, Bandy-legs, Spindle-shanks, Snub-nose, Red-top, and so on for five hundred more.

But to all of them the little man shouted:

"Ho, ho! No, no, my Royal Dame!
That's not my name; that's not
   my name."

The third day the last of the messengers came back weary and worn from his long journey and said: "Forgive me, sorrowful Queen. I could find no new name but one. Yesterday as I was passing through a strange wood, I saw a tiny, red-roofed hut and in the dooryard there capered a funny little man who sang:

'To-day I bake; to-morrow I brew;
To-day for one; to-morrow for two.
For how should she learn, poor
   Royal Dame,
That Rumpel-stilt-skin is my name?'"

When the Queen heard this, she surprised the messenger by a peal of laughter, for she knew the singer must have been her little gold-spinner. So, when at sunset he came skipping in and said: "Tell me my name if you can," she asked, putting on a doleful look and clasping her baby to her breast: "Is it Hans?"

"No."

"Is it Fritz?"

"No."

"Well then, it's Rumpel-stilt-skin."

"The fairies have told you! The fairies have told you!" shrieked the little man in a rage, and he stamped his right foot so deep down through the floor that he could not pull it out. Becoming more angry still, he laid hold of his left foot with both hands and jerked so hard that he split himself in two, for he was really made of gingerbread, as all Rumpel-stilt-skins are.

TOADS AND DIAMONDS

Once upon a time there was a widow who had two daughters. The elder was just like her mother in face and in disposition, and both were so disobliging and so rude that there was no living with them. The younger took after her father, who had been the kindest, sweetest-tempered of men, and she was, besides, one of the most beautiful girls that the sun ever looked upon.

As people naturally love those in whom they see themselves, this mother was foolishly fond of her elder daughter and almost hated the younger. She made her eat in the kitchen and work from daylight till dark.

Among other tasks the child had to go twice a day to a spring over a mile and a half from the house and bring home a heavy clay pitcher full of water.

One morning as she stood resting a minute by the fountain, an old woman hobbled up to her. "Please, my bonny lass," she begged, "give me a drink."

"Oh, yes, with all my heart, Goody," said the kind little girl. Then she rinsed out her pitcher, caught the clear, cool water just as it came bubbling from the rock, and held up the pitcher that the old woman might drink more easily.

Refreshed by the sweet water, the beggar leaned on her staff and said to the child: "You are so kind to an old woman, my dear, and so good and so mannerly, that I have a gift for you." For this was a fairy, who had taken the form of a shabby old cripple to see whether this pretty girl was as sweet as she looked. "This shall be the gift," went on the fairy: "At every word you speak there shall come out of your mouth a flower or a jewel."

When the girl reached home, her mother scolded her for staying so long at the fountain. "Please forgive me, dear mother," pleaded the child. And as she spoke there fell from her lips two blush roses, two lovely pearls, and one big, sparkling diamond.

"What is this? What is this?" cried the mother, treading on the roses in her eagerness to pick up the gems. "Am I bewitched or did I really see these pearls and this diamond fall from your mouth? What does it mean, my child?" This was the first time she had ever spoken to her younger daughter so tenderly.

The girl told her all that had happened, and at every word a ruby, an emerald, a sapphire, or a beautiful flower fell from her lips.

"As I live," cried the mother, "I must send my other daughter to the fountain. See, my precious, what comes out of your sister's mouth when she speaks. Would you not like, my pet, to have the same wonderful gift given to you? You need only go to the fountain, and when a poor old woman asks you for a drink, give it to her very politely."

"Do I look like a servant?" cried the rude girl. "Is it fit for me to carry a heavy pitcher to the spring for water?"

"Indeed and you shall go, you minx," snapped her mother, "and go this instant."

Angrily the girl snatched up the best silver pitcher, her mother's wedding pitcher that never went to the well, and set forth grumbling and muttering.

As she stood by the fountain she saw coming out of the woods a lady in a dress that seemed woven out of rainbows. This was the same fairy who had been so generous to the younger sister, but of course Miss Cross-Patch, waiting impatiently for a poor old woman, did not know that.

"Will you give me a drink, my dear?" asked the lady.

"And why should *I* draw water for *you?*" was the saucy answer. "Here is the pitcher, you may stoop down and dip up water for yourself."

"Are these your best manners?" asked the fairy as gently as before. "This, then, must be your gift, since you are so rude and so unkind: At every word you speak there shall drop out of your mouth a snake or a toad."

As soon as the mother saw her favorite coming, she held out her hands to catch the jewels, crying: "Speak, daughter! Speak!"

"Speak what?" answered the girl pettishly. And with the words there dropped from her mouth a toad and a viper.

"Mercy on us!" gasped the mother. "What horrors have we here? You wretch," she screamed, turning to the younger sister, "you are the cause of this, and you shall pay for it, you shall, you shall!" She rushed in fury at the child, who slipped through the door, fled away, and hid in the forest.

That evening the King's son, riding through the woods, heard sobbing and found her crying in a hawthorn thicket. "My pretty maid," he said, leaning from his saddle, "why are you here alone when night is coming on?"

"Oh, sir," replied the girl, "my mother has turned me out of doors."

The Prince was amazed when he saw five pearls and diamonds fall shining from her mouth. "What does this mean?" he cried. "Tell me all that has happened."

So with all manner of flowers and jewels slipping from her lips as she talked, she told him the whole story, and he fell in love with her while she was telling it.

"To be sure," he said to himself, "my father meant me to wed a king's daughter, but such a rain of precious stones is greater treasure than the marriage portion I should receive with any princess, however wealthy." So the King's son led the maiden to the royal palace and there they were married amid great rejoicing.

As for her sister, she was so hateful that her own mother turned her off, and the miserable girl, having wandered about a good while without finding any one to take her in, went to a corner in the wood and there lived as queen of the toads and vipers.